MALONE

And The Mad Bad Inventor

MIMA MALONE AND THE MAD BAD INVENTOR

Text copyright © 2020 Kate Poels
Illustration copyright © 2020 Jag Lall

ISBN-13: 9798667221579

For my amazing parents who have always read
every word.

Happy reading!
with love
Kate Poels
xx

Chapter 1

Blue Tongues and Bald Children

J uno Jermy is missing!
Yesterday she was sitting by me in history making me laugh with a really amazing impression of King Henry VIII. This morning she didn't show up for registration and, when Mr McLachlan in the office called her mum, she said Juno left the house like normal to walk to school.

The reason I know all this is because Miss Barker, our head teacher, called me into her office with a bunch of other children from my class to ask us if we know where she could be.

'I want you to think very carefully,' Miss Barker says. 'Perhaps you can think of anywhere she might have gone, or even why she might not have wanted to come to school today.'

Juno is the sort of girl who absolutely hates getting into trouble. She once ran into the toilets crying when a supply teacher told her off for using pen in her maths book... even though she has such amazing neat work and Mrs Rees had already told her it was fine. She never has dirty uniform and always remembers to bring her reading journal to school EVERY DAY! Juno is completely and totally NOT the sort of girl who leaves for school in the morning and decides to go off somewhere else for the day.

'She might've gone into town to McPhizz's Sweet Emporium,' suggests my friend Siddharth. 'It's their one month anniversary and Cherry McPhizz is giving away free sweets to celebrate all day.'

'No,' I say. 'That's probably where you'd go Sid but Juno wouldn't skip school to go to a sweet shop. She wouldn't skip school for anything.'

Miss Barker nods.

'Yes Jemima, I think you're probably right,' she says and pushes her fingers into the sides of her head in the way grown-ups sometimes do when they're thinking so hard their brain starts aching.

'Thank you for your help children,' she says. 'Now back to class everyone please. I will let you know if there's any news.'

As we're leaving her office, we see a police car pull up outside the front door. Two police officers buzz to be let in and they look pretty grim. I hope it's not bad news.

***

2

I am *really* worried about Juno and not just because she's missing but because of how she might be when she comes back.

You see, Juno isn't the first child to have gone missing from around here. A couple of weeks ago Davey Donna, the coolest boy in Year 5, disappeared too. He was only missing for a couple of hours before Mrs Yap, the lady from the Chinese restaurant down the road, found him behind her car when she went to put the rubbish out. Davey was curled up like a baby, fast asleep and sucking his thumb. When Mrs Yap woke him up, he started howling like a hungry piglet and didn't stop until his mum came to collect him. Since then he hasn't been quite right and he is definitely NOT the coolest boy in Year 5 anymore.

'Do you think she'll turn up soon?' Sid asks me on the way back to the classroom.

'I hope so,' I tell him. 'And I hope when she does, nothing weird has happened to her like Davey or Amos or Amelie.'

Amos De La Harpe and Amelie Vigh didn't actually disappear but strange things have still happened to them. Amelie now clucks like a chicken every time she hears her name and Amos came to school on Monday and wouldn't talk to anyone. Not even the teachers. He managed to keep his mouth shut for the whole morning, right up until break time when Billy Belcher, the meanest boy in school, stamped on his toe for no good reason. Amos yowled really loudly and we could all see that the inside of his

3

mouth was completely BLUE! His tongue and every single one of his teeth were the colour of the cleaner our caretaker sticks down the loo.

So, with all the weird things that are happening to children round here, I think we really do need to be worried about Juno even though she hasn't been missing for all that long yet.

Chapter 2

The Great Toe Mystery

M aths is never my favourite subject even though I sit on a table with my best friends, Daisy, Sid and Olivia. But today it's even worse because none of us can think about multiplying bags of oranges by monkeys in the zoo when Juno is still missing.

'Do you think she's been abducted by aliens?' Sid asks.

'Of course not,' snaps Olivia.

'I hope she doesn't start making animal noises,' I say. 'Or having spit she could write with.'

Mrs Rees, our teacher, usually tells us off when we chat in class but she's not really paying attention today either.

Eventually she tells us to put our maths books away and she puts YouTube on instead. Some children cheer but they soon stop when we find out we're

5

watching an educational film about the life cycle of frogs.

We are just at the bit where the froglets lose their tails when the classroom door opens and Juno comes in. I give a little whoop to see her and check for any signs of weirdness. So far, nothing strange apart from her being really late

'Juno!' cries Mrs Rees. 'Whatever happened to you?'

'Nothing Miss,' says Juno, going a bit pink because she doesn't really like everyone looking at her. 'I thought I left home early today but when I got here the gates were already locked. I came by the office but Mr McLachlan looked a bit busy with the police so I just signed myself in. Is that ok?' She's looking really uncomfortable.

'But it's just about break time,' says Mrs Rees.

'Is it?' says Juno, looking a bit confused. She looks at the clock on the wall above the door and her eyes open wide. Then she sits down hard in her chair.

'Right, everyone else you can go out to break a bit early today whilst I take Juno up to see Miss Barker.'

'I'm really sorry,' sobs Juno. 'I really didn't mean to be so late. I remember feeling a bit tired and then sitting down by someone's wall but I didn't think I'd been there for more than a few minutes. I must have just fallen asleep.'

'You're not in trouble dear,' says Mrs Rees kindly. 'But your parents and the police will want to know you've turned up and you're safe and well. They've been so

6

worried about you and they'll want to try and find out what happened.'

As soon as she gets back from Miss Barker's office, everybody in the entire school crowds around to find out what happened to her but she can't remember anything at all. I'm very pleased there is no sign of a blue mouth and, when I say her name, she doesn't start to make animal noises so maybe Juno is alright after all

In the afternoon we all take our school shoes off and put on those stupid pinchy black pumps we have to wear for indoor PE. Juno sits next to me and so it's me who first notices that something HAS happened to her. When she peels off her white school socks, I can't help spotting a very big problem.

'Juno!' I shriek. 'What happened to your toes?'

I feel a bit guilty then because my shrieking has made everyone in the class turn around to see what's going on. Juno looks down at her feet and shrieks even louder than I did when she sees that her toes have got big flaps of skin between them now which definitely didn't used to be there. They look like frog feet, only obviously not green or slimy.   Mrs Rees comes over to calm everyone down but she gulps so hard when she sees Juno's feet that I think she might be trying hard not to shriek herself.

'Juno dear, put your shoes back on,' she says as calmly as she can.

'Daisy, go up to the office and ask Mr McLachlan to call Juno's mother. Tell him it's very important and she

7

needs to come to school as soon as possible to collect her.'

Daisy always gets chosen for important jobs because she's the most sensible person in our class. She's also the best at maths, has the neatest handwriting and, back when we were in the infants, she was the first person to finish all the colour coded reading books and move on to real books from the library.

Juno packs her things up silently and goes up to the office to wait with Mr McLachlan until her mum arrives.

The rest of us still have to do P.E so I can't talk to Daisy and the others until it's time to go home.

Daisy and I have been best friends for a very long time, since before we could really talk. We went to toddler group together then pre-school and now we've been in the same class at school for five years and two terms. She lives at the back of my garden. That's not as weird as it sounds, it's just that her house has a garden that backs onto ours so we're back to back neighbours. We've built a tunnel through our hedges so we can visit without ever having to go out onto the road.

Sid and Olivia live really close to us as well and, now that we're in Year 5, our mums let the four of us walk home together.

Today we walk home slowly as we have lots to talk about.

'What do you think happened to Juno?' I ask

Daisy.

'I have no idea at all,' says Daisy which makes me nervous because Daisy *always* knows about *everything*.

'I think it was most probably aliens,' says Sid, who is totally obsessed with aliens. This is ever since he read a book about how they can come and take over the lives of normal humans. Now he's just waiting for it to happen and secretly hoping that, when they do come, they'll pick him.

'Seriously Sid,' I say, poking him in the ribs.

'I am being serious,' says Sid. 'It has to be aliens. There's no other explanation.'

'What about her webbed feet?' I ask, ignoring him. 'That was really weird.'

'My aunty's brother has webbed feet,' says Olivia. 'It hasn't done him any harm. I think he's quite proud of them actually. He likes to show them off whenever we see him.'

'Yes, but we know Juno didn't have them yesterday,' says Daisy. 'And things like this don't just happen overnight.'

'Did you notice her eyes?' asks Olivia.

We all shake our heads waiting for Olivia to tell us what we hadn't noticed. Olivia is pretty quiet and really shy but she's absolutely brilliant at spotting all the tiny things nobody else does. She would make a completely fantastic spy or detective.

'They were really bright and watery,' she tells us. 'Just like Amos's were when he started to cluck like a chicken.'

'So they must be linked,' says Daisy.

'Hmm,' says Sid, stroking his chin thoughtfully. 'Taken by the same alien.'

'Enough about aliens,' I say.

'You'll see I'm right one day,' he replies, opening his garden gate and walking up to his house. He stops just before the front door.

'Watch out for aliens!' he calls before going inside.

Daisy never goes back home to her own road. She always walks home with me and Olivia. Then Olivia carries on up the road to her house and Daisy goes through the hedge tunnel in my back garden to hers.

'I don't know what's going on,' she says. She looks a bit worried and that always makes me worried too.

'It's very weird and getting creepier too,' I say. 'What should we do?'

'Just be careful,' she says and then disappears through the hedge.

Chapter 3

Dog Poo Shoe

It's been almost two weeks since Juno disappeared and then turned up again. She's now absolutely fine and doesn't really mind the whole webbed toe thing. She says it makes swimming easy and she's going to sign up for the club gala.

Juno might think everything's okay again but nobody else does. The grown-ups are all getting jittery and trying to get to the bottom of whatever is happening to the kids in our town. Last week, we all had leaflets pushed through our doors telling us that the scientists believe the most likely cause is some kind of weird bug. They don't know where it comes from but tests so far show that it isn't contagious. We're meant to boil all water before we drink it, stay away from the river and cook all food properly. Sealed food is fine but fresh fruit and vegetables are 'high risk' so shouldn't be eaten raw until further notice. We must wash our hands whenever we can, oh and the three second rule is now illegal.

But I don't think they know anything for sure. As well as all the information about super bugs, there are posters turning up all over the town telling us to BE ALERT and TRAVEL IN GROUPS.

In assembly Miss Barker is joined by a policeman called PC Blinkered who talks to us about *stranger danger* and what to do if we think we're being followed.

He gives us a list of rules like:

Always tell a grown-up where you are going.

Never speak to a stranger.

Never take money, food or gifts from a stranger.

'What about the tooth fairy?' Yasmeena in Year 2 asks. 'Shouldn't I put my tooth under my pillow because I don't really know the tooth fairy?'

'I think the tooth fairy is probably safe,' Miss Barker says with a reassuring smile.

'When I was in Ireland, I heard there are lots of evil fairies,' says Jensen in Year 4. 'So maybe we should all be careful about where we put our teeth.'

'Perhaps if anyone is worried then they could leave their teeth somewhere else for now.' Miss Barker says. 'PC Blinkered, do carry on.'

But before he has a chance, Katinka in Year 3 shouts out, 'What about Father Christmas?'

She asks her question without putting her hand up first which makes all the teachers look at her crossly. But she carries on anyway. 'He's a stranger too really so do you think we should all hang our stockings up outside this year?'

PC Blinkered looks a bit surprised.

'It's the end of June,' he says. 'So, nobody should really worry about where to hang their stockings just yet.'

Then half the infants start to cry because they think Father Christmas might be involved in all the weird things that are going on but Mrs Gogerty, the Year 1 teacher, stands up to calm everything down by pointing out that Father Christmas has been delivering presents to many, many children for many, many years and nothing strange has happened to any of them. She also points out that this is true for the tooth fairy too and that both are therefore beyond suspicion.

PC Blinkered has no idea what else to say so he just hands out cards to everyone with a list of rules on one side. On the other side is a number to call if anyone has information or worries about what is going on in our home town.

***

There's only been one more victim of 'Operation Weird' since Juno's feet webbed themselves.

Last week, Humza Morgan wouldn't take his hat off in registration. It was a really hot day but he said he had a head cold and the doctor said he couldn't let it get any colder. Mrs Rees said that he was being ridiculous and if he didn't have a proper note from his doctor then he couldn't keep his hat on inside. When he took the hat off, the whole class gasped in shock because there was not one hair left on his head. His scalp was so polished and shiny that the rays from the light bulb above him bounced right off. He didn't look bad really. My Uncle Guy is bald and I think it really suits him. It's just that we hadn't expected it and Humza did *not* look as though he'd done it on purpose and he certainly *didn't* seem happy about his new look.

***

Like most of the kids in our school I'm now on high alert for strangers waiting to offer me money, treats and presents just so they can lure me away and turn my hair green or something. But, so far, I haven't spotted anything out of the ordinary. Every morning, before I leave for school, Mum reminds me that I'm not allowed to walk anywhere without at least one of my friends and that she wants to know where I am all the time.

'Bye pumpkin,' she calls as I leave the house.

I wave over my shoulder as I go through the gate and latch it behind me. But I don't look where I'm going, or where I'm putting my feet.

SQUELCH!

I step in the biggest, smelliest dog poo and it squidges right up the toe of my school shoes.

'Urghh!' I say, trying to rub it off on the side of the pavement.

Then I hear the worst voice in the world shout

something that turns my day on its head and my life inside out.

'Oi, Squirt-Brain! Guess who's just moved in next door?'

The voice belongs to Billy Belcher who's sitting on the wall of the house next to mine. The house that used to belong to lovely Mr and Mrs Custard until they moved to Zanzibar about two months ago. Since then it's had a big FOR SALE sign in the garden and I'd been excited about who might be about to move in and be our new neighbours.

Billy is now holding the FOR SALE sign and using it to poke at something on the floor by his feet. He's the very last person in the world I would have voted for as my new neighbour.   Everyone in the whole school knows about Billy Belcher and we all try to stay out of his way because he's a complete nutter and really evil. When he walks past someone he often gives them a punch on their arm or a slap on the back of their head for no reason. I heard that once he even threw Parmeet from Year 2 in the wheelie bin because he accidentally bumped into him on the way out to break.

'What's the matter Squirt Brain?' he says. 'Aren't you going to welcome me to Howahorse Road?

I take a step closer thinking I should try and be nice and make an effort to get on with Billy. It would definitely make living next to him a bit easier if we could at least be pleasant to each other.

'Welcome to the street,' I say quietly.

'Nah,' he says. 'On second thoughts don't come any closer. You really stink of dog poo.'

Then he jumps off the wall and waves his hand around his nose as though he's swatting away actual stink waves.

Just then, an enormous lorry and a pretty big van drive down the road and stop right by Billy.

'It's been fun smelling you,' Billy calls after me.

'Touch nothing in the van,' a loud voice shouts and a man wearing a green coat and huge glasses runs over to the lorry. 'You are just to unpack the furniture from the lorry but the van is full of... um ... fragile and delicate antiques. Do NOT touch them.'

So it's really happening. As I leave the removal people to fill the house next door up with Billy Belcher's stuff, I feel gloomy.

I love my street. Howahorse Road is the best place to live and I should know because I've lived here all my life. It doesn't lead anywhere so there aren't loads of cars driving up and down it all the time. This means all the children who live on our street can go out on Sunday afternoons and ride bikes or scooters up and down whilst some of the dads sit on deckchairs pretending to keep an eye on us. Really, they're just drinking beer and talking about the rugby or the football or the golf.

It's also really handy because all my best friends are close by. Olivia lives at number twelve, Sid lives at number forty-six and I'm right in the middle of them. My house is number thirty-three. And, of course, Daisy is my

16

back to back neighbour so really it's just about perfect.

Or it used to be. But now that Billy Belcher has moved in next door, I think things are going to get ugly.

Chapter 4

The Problem with an Arty-Party Mum

Billy thinks it's brilliant fun to tell everyone about the dog poo on the shoe thing and so I take any opportunity to hide from him and anyone else who wants to tease me about it.

It's Daisy and my turn to look after Margaret De Belvoir Bouffant Burgh, or Mags, this week. She's the school guinea-pig and she lives in a cage in the library. We take extra time to clean her cage out because it keeps me out of the playground and away from the poo teasers.

Feeding Mags is the fun part. We collect dandelion leaves from outside the Year 1 classrooms and hold them in front of her. She grabs the end with her hooked front teeth and pulls it in a bit a time whilst her mouth moves even quicker than my big sister Betsy when she's gossiping on the phone. I reckon she'd be brilliant in a strawberry lace race.

Grooming her is also really fun. There's a special

brush that sits on top of her cage and she has a LOT of long black and white fur that needs to stay tangle free.

There's one job nobody likes much though and that's cleaning out the stinking sawdust heap. Mags can make an enormous amount of poo for such a small animal. It's just my luck that I'm in the middle of sweeping all the revolting mess into the compost bucket when three boys from 6CR, my class, come in to change their library books.

'Is that stink coming from the guinea-pig or your shoe?' one of them says.

'Bet you love this job don't you,' says his friend. 'Gives you more chance to play with poo.'

They all laugh like it's the funniest thing they've ever heard and I can feel myself going red. Mrs Clarke, our lovely librarian gets up from the desk she was working at and comes over to us.

'Poo jokes?' she says. 'If that's the sort of thing you're interested in boys then I'm sure I can find some books to make you laugh.'

She walks over to the 'new readers' shelves for the infants and starts flicking through the books there.

'Yeah well...' says the first boy.

'Sorry Mrs Clarke...' says the second boy.

'Come on...'says the third and they all leave their books on the *returns* trolley and walk off.

'Thank you,' I say.

Mrs Clarke smiles then winks.

'It seems they weren't so keen on my choices after

all,' she says.

***

When I get home I just want to slop onto the sofa and forget everything, but my big sister has other plans for me.

'There you are Mima. Have you fed Catt yet?' Betsy asks as soon as I walk into the house. Betsy and I named our dog after our favourite cousin whose name is Catherine. When we were little, we thought that was a stupid name for a dog. So, we called her Catt for short. It might be a bit weird but it stuck and now it's the only name she's got.

'How can I have fed her?' I say. 'I've only just got in.'

'Well make sure you do.'

'Alright, Bossy Knickers.' I mumble but I get out the dog food as Catt is looking at me with eyes that can't be left unfed. When I tip the food into her bowl, I feel a softness curl around my legs.

'Hello Pyjamas, you're next,' I tell our cat as I squidge his food out of the pouch in a stinking dollop.

'Mum's on one of her arty farty courses so I'm in charge,' Betsy says, pointing to a sticky note on the fridge.

The sticky note unfortunately does say that Betsy is in charge. It also says that there's some left-over salami casserole in the fridge which we can pad out with a tin of tuna fish and some sweetcorn for our supper.

Mum would never win any cookery competition, unless the prize went to the weirdest dish. She usually looks in the fridge and then the cupboard, sees what needs using up and either throws it all in the frying pan with an egg or sticks it in the oven with a can of tomatoes and calls it casserole.

I love my mum very much but she's definitely one of the most embarrassing people I know. I blame Granny and Grandpops who had her in the 1970's when it was cool and 'hippy' to give your children bonkers names. They called her *Rainbow Waterfall,* although everyone now shortens it to *Bow* but even so it's a bit weird. If you give a baby a weird name then you can't really blame them when they grow up into a person who likes wearing vintage clothes with bright colours and huge patterns. Or who has about ten million scarves which always dangle in her fruit tea. Or who insists on filling the house with strange arty-crafty things she makes at workshops.

She's utterly mad but I love her to bits. I'm not totally one hundred percent sure I can say the same thing about my sister. She used to be quite nice and I think I can almost remember her being kind to me... but then she had a birthday. It was her thirteenth birthday and it changed her forever. Betsy has now officially decided she doesn't count as *'children'* anymore and that means she can't play *'stupid baby games'* with me. Mum says it's just a phase and I'll go through it too when I'm a teenager. But I know she's wrong. I'll never be like Betsy.

'After you've fed Catt and Pyjamas you need to

tidy away all your books and set the table for supper,' she calls. 'Then there's a pile of washing Mum wants sorting so you can do that too.'

When Betsy's left in charge, she thinks that means she can boss me around and make me do anything she wants. Don't worry I never do it. Or if I do then I make sure I get things really wrong like the time I polished her black shoes with Mum's bright red shoe polish and she had to go to school looking like Minnie Mouse.

'I've got homework,' I tell her and run up the stairs singing loudly to block out her grumpy grunts.

As soon as I get in my room, I notice noises coming from the back garden. Loud, growly noises that are very new to Howahorse Road. I look out of my bedroom window and see that my garden is empty. I live in the attic and I get a really brilliant view into several other gardens along our road as well as ours, so I can see that the noise is coming from next door. Billy Belcher is in his garden with the nastiest looking dog I think I've ever seen. I love all animals but not ones that sound like this or ones that have mean teeth and sharp eyes like the one in Billy's garden. If Billy Belcher was a dog then he would be just like the one he's now playing with. Well I say playing but it's actually more like fighting by the looks of it.

He looks up and I duck away from the window fast. I can't see him anymore but I can still hear him and that awful fanged dog. Also, I can hear something else really strange. It's coming from the chimney that goes up

22

between our house and next door and it sounds like when mum is cooking pasta and then goes off to finish wrapping an old chair in ribbon or something and forgets all about it. Then the water bubbles crossly and spills right out of the pan, hissing when it hits the cooker.

I put my ear to the chimney and there's no doubt about it. The bubbling, hissing, spitting noises are coming from the other side. What in the name of strawberry laces are they doing next door?

I don't have a chance to think about the noise anymore because my walkie-talkie is beeping which means Daisy needs something. I pick it up and press the button.

'Mima Bear receiving. Go ahead, Sunny Daise. Over.'

'Hello Mima Bear. *Cheese and ham toastie*... I repeat *Cheese and ham toastie*. Over.'

"*Cheese and ham toastie*" is our top-secret emergency code. It means something big has happened and we have to talk face to face.

'Roger that, Sunny Daise.' I say. 'Meet you at the Purple Turtle in five minutes. Over.'

'Make it two.' Daisy says. 'Over and out.'

The Purple Turtle is the name of our club house at the back of Daisy's garden. It's an old plastic play house she had for her fourth birthday, a bit small for us now but it still does the job and it's completely private. I creep downstairs, past Betsy who's sitting on the big chair with her legs curled up, STILL talking to somebody on her

23

phone. She doesn't notice as I sneak out into the back garden and through the hedge tunnel. Daisy is already there.

'Crikey Bikey Daisy,' I say. 'Are you ill?' I only saw her only a few hours ago but in that tiny time something huge has happened.

Daisy's eyes are extra bright and watery, and her face and neck are completely covered in little green spots.

Chapter 5

Can Houses Really Flash?

I can't help staring at the spots.

'Is it sore?' I ask Daisy.

'No, just a bit itchy really,' says Daisy.

'You didn't eat the rest of those really old chocolates we found at the back of your mum's cupboard, did you?' I check.

'Ummm...' Daisy says, looking sheepish.

'Oh, Daisy you didn't?' I say. 'They were years out of date!'

'It can't be that,' Daisy says, blushing pink which makes her spots look even greener. 'I only tasted the end of one and it was disgusting so I spat it out straight away. Besides, that was weeks ago.'

'So, what is it then?'

'I don't know. I've stuck to all the rules, kept my hands clean and been careful with everything I've eaten.'

'You were fine at lunch time when we were

cleaning out Mags' Cage,' I say.

'Mum came to pick me up early for the dentist but he was running late. By the time we finished it wasn't worth going back to school so we just came straight home. I was really tired so I had a quick nap and when I woke up...'

'You looked like this,' I finish and Daisy nods sadly.

'Don't worry, Daise,' I say. 'We'll get to the bottom of this.'

Daisy's mum calls from the house to say she has an emergency appointment for her at the doctors and she has to get ready to go.

'Good luck,' I tell her before she runs up the garden to her house.

I sit in the Purple Turtle for a little while after Daisy has left. Something very weird is going on in our town and I have to admit I'm pretty scared. We've always been taught to tell a responsible adult when there's a problem. But right now, the adults are running around like Catt when she's chasing her tail. None of them have a clue what's going on and they keep going around in circles without actually getting anywhere. It's all very well sticking up a few posters and telling us to stay away from strangers but what good is that if they don't know who, or what, is making all these weird things happen and how to stop them?

I decide that I'm not going to leave it up to the grown-ups. Adults are great at dealing with what they know about but I've noticed they only look at the obvious

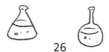

26

or the most likely. There is nothing obvious or likely about blue teeth, green spots or sudden chicken impressions. So, it stands to reason adults are probably not the best people to be doing this investigation.

They think this is all down to some strange bug that's sweeping our town. But I think it's more sinister and dangerous than that. If it's a bug then how come it's just targeting the kids? So far, every single victim has been between seven and thirteen. This is no coincidence. I think someone is doing this on purpose and I'm going to find out exactly who it is and what is going on before more crazy things happen.

***

Daisy walkie-talkies me as soon as she gets back to tell me that the doctor doesn't know what's wrong with her. She thinks it might be a weird skin allergy so she gave Daisy some medicine to take and said she hoped the spots would be gone by the morning.

But they haven't gone. Daisy is still covered in green spots so her mum tells her she can have a day off school to see if they get better.

Luckily Billy Belcher isn't outside his house when I leave for school. As I walk past, I can't help glancing over just to make sure he isn't lurking somewhere. And then something EXTREMELY weird happens. I swear on Catt's furry life that the entire house flashes! Yes...actually lights up like a giant Christmas decoration. All the

27

windows shine bright green and then it's back to normal.

'Everything alright, dearie?' calls Mrs Tattle, the nosiest person who lives on Howahorse Road.

'Yes.' I say. 'Well I think so at least. It's just that...well...did you see anything strange just happen to that house?'

'Strange you ask?' says Mrs Tattle, rubbing her chin and peering over her glasses to look at the house.

'I swear that house just flashed,' I say, staring at it in case it does it again.

'Maybe a flash of lightning?' she suggests.

I look up at the blue, cloudless sky and shake my head.

'No,' Mrs Tattle says. 'Well perhaps one of the street lamps flickered, or maybe a trick of the eye.'

'Maybe,' I say, beginning to wonder the same thing myself.

'It's exciting to have the professor move into our little street isn't it?'

'The professor?' I ask her, not quite sure what she's talking about.

'Well yes. Professor Barrington Belcher, esteemed inventor and a bit of a celebrity in the scientific world. What he doesn't know about chemistry, physics and biology is quite frankly probably not worth knowing in the first place.'

Awful Billy Belcher has a super-dad? How can someone as brain-squished as Billy have a dad who is a scientific inventor of brilliant stuff?

'Are you coming, Mima?' Olivia calls as she walks past on the other side of the road.

'Nice to talk to you Mrs Tattle,' I say and hurry after Olivia, feeling quite glad to get away. I look over my shoulder as we leave and see Mrs Tattle watching the Belchers' house. I hope it flashes again but nothing happens.

Then, as we walk further down Howahorse Road, a van drives past. On the side of the van in bright green letters are the words:

THE WRENCHITT CLINIC - PRIVATE DENTAL CARE

'Olivia, look!' I say and we watch the van drive on until it stops outside Number 31. The Belchers' house.

I'm desperate to talk to the others about what's going on and I wait until Sid joins us. But then, as we reach the end of Howahorse Road, another person dressed in our school uniform jumps out.

'Lucky me,' Billy Belcher says. 'Looks like I don't have to walk to school on my own this morning.' He gives us one of his horrid, crooked, fangy grins and then punches us all on the arm.

Chapter 6

Stinky Emergency Meeting

At lunch time, I take Sid and Olivia to a corner of the playground where we can talk without worrying about anyone hearing. It's a dead space tucked away between the boys' toilet block and the rails we can lock our bikes or scooters to. It's the part of the playground that must have the sewage pipes running underneath because it always stinks and you have to try and breathe in as little as possible. People don't go there unless they have to because it smells so bad. But that's exactly why it's the best place to go if you need to hold a *secret* meeting.

'We need a plan,' I say, although it sounds more like 'be deed a pan,' because I'm pinching my nose.

'Bot did oo say?' asks Sid, pinching his own nose.

'I said be deed a pan,' I repeat crossly.

'I cart ubbersad oo,' says Sid, also getting cross.

Olivia gets out a pack of tissues and hands them

around and we all make nose plugs to stick up our nostrils and stop the smell getting in so we can talk properly.

'That's better,' I say. 'There's something really strange going on here and I don't think it has anything to do with a weird super bug.'

'You're right,' says Sid. 'It's not just a weird super bug. It's a weird, mutated, alien super bug.'

'No Sid,' I say, trying to stay calm. 'I don't think this has anything to do with *any* sort of bug.'

'I agree,' says Olivia. 'I've been wondering. If it was a bug then how come the adults and the really little kids are okay?'

'Yes!' I say. 'It's only school kids and I think that is highly suspicious.'

Olivia takes a little notepad and a glittery pen from her bag.

'We need to begin an investigation,' she says.

To be honest, I'm a bit put out. This was supposed to be my big moment and now Olivia has jumped in as chief investigator. I'm also jealous of her investigation pad and make a mental note to sort one out for myself.

'So, what are the clues?' Olivia asks and I forget about who's in charge and remember Daisy and why it's important we get on with the investigation.

I tell Sid and Olivia about Daisy's green spots and Billy Belcher's professor dad.

'Very suspicious,' Olivia says and writes something in her pad.

'And then there's the dentist,' she says. 'Mr

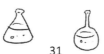

31

Wrenchitt.'

'That's right,' I say.

'I still don't get it,' says Sid, wrinkling up his nose despite the tissue nose plugs.

'Daisy got her green spots after she came back from the dentist. The same dentist who was last seen in the house of an inventor,' I tell him. 'A house which flashes bright green now and again,' I add. 'I saw it this morning.'

I see a look pass between Sid and Olivia.

'Hey!' I cry. 'You don't believe me, do you?'

'It does sound a bit weird,' Sid admits.

'Of course we believe you,' Olivia says but the little twitch around her cheeks tell me she's lying because they always twitch when she fibs.

'Well fine then,' I snap.

I fiddle with the toggles on my hood and pull them tight together so that I disappear inside a furry den.

Sid's eye peeks into the tiny gap I've left.

'Humph,' I grump but I know I won't be able to stay cross for very long.

A long, brown finger pokes through the gap and prods my chin again and again.

'Sid, get off!'

'Well stop being a stropper then and get back to business,' Sid says whilst his finger is still poking my chin.

I shrug my hood off and pretend to snap at his finger.

'What's the plan Mima?' Olivia asks, pen ready to

jot everything down.

'The first thing we need to do is find out how many of the KAWs saw Mr Wrenchitt before they started acting strange,' I say.

'What are KAWs?' Sid asks and I'm pleased because it shows he's listening AND it gives me a chance to explain the very clever and detective-type name that I made up.

'KAWs are what we're going to be calling the Kids who Act Weirdly from now on,' I tell them.

Olivia and Sid don't look as impressed as I think they should.

'Why?' Sid asks.

'It's called short hand Sid and it's what all the best detectives do,' I say, a bit snappily. 'We need to make a list of KAWs and check if any of them also went to the dentist. If they all did then we know it's him and we can tell the police to go and investigate.'

Everyone agrees and Olivia writes down all the names of the kids at our school who have gone weird. There are nine in all, not including Daisy, so we take three each and begin our mission to speak to them all by the end of the day. Sid has swimming straight after school but, when he's finished, we're all going to meet back at my house to go through the lists. I'm so completely sure we'll find a link between the KAWs and Mr Wrenchitt.

There are still ten minutes left of break so I decide to see if I can tick off the first KAW on my list.

Davey Donna is sitting on a bench eating his snack.

He's on his own which is a bonus so I go over and sit down next to him.

'Do you mind if I ask you a few questions?' I ask him.

'Okay,' he says, although he doesn't sound too sure about it.

'I'm just doing some research on...um...dentists,' I say. 'For a project I'm working on.'

'Okay,' he says again.

'Which dentist do you go to?' I ask.

'He looks a bit baffled but answers me anyway. 'Mr Wrenchitt, on Bridge Street.'

'Hmmm, interesting.' I say trying not to let my face show signs of excitement. 'And when did you last visit the dentist?'

'It was about three weeks ago,' he says. 'The day before I... when I... you know, behind the Chinese restaurant...'

He looks as though he's about to cry but then he sticks his thumb in his mouth and his face relaxes.

I have all the information I need. And it's just as I expected.

'Thank you very much for your time,' I say and leave Davey to finish his snack in peace.

At lunch time, I find the other two KAWs on my list but neither of them have anything useful to tell me. They haven't been to the dentist for ages and they can't remember doing anything out of the ordinary before they became KAWs.

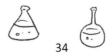

Then, just as the bell goes to signal the end of lunchtime, a girl called Kirstyn runs over to me.

'You're investigating the weird things going on around here aren't you?' she asks.

'Well,' I say cagily, 'I'm not sure *investigating* is the right word... just interested shall we say. Why? Do you have information?'

'Yes I do,' Kirstyn whispers close to my ear. 'It's not just kids you know.'

'What?'

'It's not just kids. Nibbles, my bunny, escaped yesterday, which is weird because she's never done that before.'

'Right,' I say, wondering where this is going. 'I'm sorry to hear that.'

'She was gone for a few hours but when she came back, she had no teeth. Not one!'

'That is strange,' I agree.

'We took her to the vet and he x-rayed her but there's nothing left. Not one tooth in her mouth.'

'Will she be alright?' I ask.

'The vet's looking into making her a set of false teeth but until then we have to grind up all her food for her so she can eat it.'

'Kirstyn and Jemima!' Mrs Rees calls. 'The bell has gone. Time to stop chatting and get in line.

I turn to Kirstyn but she's already running off to join her class so I head back to mine.

***

After school, Sid's picked up by his mum for his swimming lesson so it's just Olivia and me walking home.

As we leave the school gate, Olivia stops and points at the bushes of the churchyard across the road.

'Look,' she says. 'Can you see that?'

Something is glinting in the bushes.

'What was that?' I ask as there's a shuffle in the bush and whatever is glinting disappears.

'It looked like a pair of binoculars to me,' she says and I'm sure she's right.

'But who's spying on the school gate?' I ask.

'Someone who's interested in knowing about the kids and watching us when we leave,' Olivia says.

If we're going to be good detectives, we cannot leave a clue like this un-investigated. The road is clear so we cross quickly and rush over to the bush. The binoculars have gone but there's a person hurrying away between the gravestones. I'd recognise that blue mac and grey perm anywhere.

'Mrs Tattle,' we both say at the same time.

Chapter 7

The Hissing Chimney

My house is usually the best for important meetings because it's in the middle of all our houses. Also, if Mum isn't at one of her arty-farty meetings or book groups or something, she's great at just leaving us alone to get on with things. Olivia has three little sisters and a baby brother which means her house is never quiet and Sid's child minder always wants to play educational games with us or teach us stuff about history or plants or cooking. Daisy's mum keeps popping in and out of Daisy's room with drinks or snacks or just to check we're okay, which is lovely but not when you need privacy for secret things.

Daisy was worried that the others might laugh at her covered in spots so she nearly didn't come. But when I told her we have investigative leads to follow and she is the brains of the operation she agreed.

'Are they really itchy?' Olivia asks her.

'Actually, I hardly notice it now,' she says. 'If I'm reading a book or busy doing something else, I can even forget they're there.'

Olivia and I catch Daisy up with everything she's missed. She looks impressed with Olivia's notebook and the investigation notes we've already made in it.

'You think Billy's Dad, Mrs Tattle and Mr Wrenchitt are all in it together?' she says.

'They have to be,' I say.

'So that's the *who* taken care of,' Daisy says. 'But what about the *how* and the *why on earth*?'

'That's what we're going to work on next,' Olivia explains.

Sid isn't here yet but I think we should get going without him because we haven't got long before Daisy and Olivia have to get home for tea.

'I talked to the kids on my list,' I begin. 'And I found out that Davey Donna DID go to the dentist the day before he disappeared!' I say excitedly.

'What about the others?' Olivia asks.

'No,' I have to confess. 'Neither of the others have been for months. What about your list?'

'Only Amelie Vigh went to see Mr Wrenchitt,' Olivia says. 'Giacomo goes to a different dentist and Amos' mum hasn't been brave enough to take him back since he bit the dentist's little mirror in half by accident. And that was two years ago.'

'That's still very suspicious,' I say.

My bedroom door opens and crashes into the

38

wardrobe next to it making it shake.

'Careful, Sid,' I yell as three of the teddies balanced on top of the wardrobe tumble off and land in a heap by his feet.

'Sorry, Mima, it's just I have to tell you something.'

'What?'

'I've just been past the Belchers' house and it flashed,' he says with a big grin. 'I saw it.'

Just then the chimney makes a huge hissing noise followed by two loud bangs. We all stare at it, waiting for something else to happen but it's gone quiet again.

'So now you believe me?' I say. 'There's definitely something *very peculiar* going on next door.'

'Yeah, sorry,' Sid says and I smile. He doesn't often say sorry.

The rest of the emergency meeting goes okay. Sid tells us that none of the KAWs he spoke to at school have visited Mr Wrenchitt recently. That means, with Daisy, only three out of the ten have the evil dentist as a link. That's enough to make him suspicious still, but not enough to be concrete evidence. We need something else.

Olivia makes a new list in her notebook. This time it's a list of people who are probably involved somehow.

Mr Wrenchitt - because several kids saw him just before they went weird.

*Professor Barrington Belcher - because he is a mad and probably bad inventor who lives in a house that flashes and has a chimney that makes really weird noises.

*Billy Belcher - because he can't possibly live in a house that flashes and makes weird noises without being involved in it all somehow. Besides he is the evilest person we know.

*Mrs Tattle - because she must have seen the house flash that morning and didn't let on, also because she knew about the professor AND she has been binocular snooping around school.

'I think we should take all the evidence to the police,' Olivia suggests.

'Don't be daft,' says Daisy. 'What evidence do we actually have?'

She's right and we all know it.

'We need a plan to get evidence,' says Sid, staring hard at the carpet.

I get out the best brain food there is to help us think. A bag of strawberry laces. We each put one end of a lace in our mouths and see how long we can keep it there. If you have a strawberry lace in your mouth then you can't speak and if you can't speak then you have to be thinking. You have to suck just the end and let the rest dangle down. But when it gets too thin it can snap so you have to keep sucking in a little bit more of the fresh lace.

It takes ages to finish a whole lace if it's done properly. And in the meantime, hopefully we will all have done some brilliant thinking and have a decent plan.

Chapter 8

Strawberry Lace Battle

The strawberry laces turn out not to be very successful. Sid gets bored of trying to think and ends up swinging his lace to slap me around the face with it. I'm actually quite glad of the distraction because my brain can't think of anything useful either. No matter how hard I try to focus, it seems to be more interested in how they make strawberry laces and if there are actually any real strawberries in them at all. I turn my head - with the lace still hanging out of my mouth - to the side to get a good run up and then I swing it at Sid but it gets stuck to his ear. The thought of eating a strawberry lace that's been stuck on Siddharth Prasadem's ear makes me feel sick so I spit it out. A bit stays hanging on his ear for a second before sliding off in a heap on the carpet.

I laugh and then Sid snorts instead of laughing so he doesn't drop his lace. Except the snort laugh makes him choke on the lace and he has to take it out anyway.

Daisy then takes hers out to tell us both off for ruining the planning and then Olivia takes hers out to say that she must be the winner because she's the last person with a strawberry lace in her mouth.

'That was rubbish,' says Olivia and she looks a bit cross. 'Didn't anyone come up with anything useful?'

'Well I think we should look at our list of suspects and then we need to stake them out. See what they're up to,' says Daisy and we all agree with her because she's usually right.

'Great idea,' I say.

'Let's begin with Mrs Tattle,' Olivia says. 'Because she's close by and also because she's not as scary as the Belchers.'

It seems like a good place to start so we all go downstairs and across the road to Mrs Tattle's house. Mrs Tattle is one of those ladies who likes to make cups of tea and offer around a tin of biscuits. She especially loves children going for a visit and my mum's always trying to get me to be a good neighbour to a lonely old woman. But to be honest, the promise of a drink and some biscuits isn't enough to make me want to go because it's so boring, so I try and wriggle out of it any time Mum starts her 'kindness to old people' nag. But right now, it does seem the easiest way to try and gather some clues.

We decide to all go together. If she invites us in for a cup of tea, then we can take it in turns to pretend to need to use her loo but really we'll be having a look around for any clues. We walk bravely up the little path in front of Mrs Tattle's house. For about a minute, we fight over who should ring the bell but eventually Sid says, 'Oh for goodness sake!' and presses the buzzer, knocking on the door for good measure.

No answer. Sid tries again and I have to say I'm relieved there are no sounds of footsteps coming from behind the door.

'Nobody's home,' I say and turn to go.

'Hang on a minute, one more try,' says Sid and he presses the bell again.

Still no answer so we all leave. And then something, I'm not sure what, makes me want to turn around and look at her house again. There, mostly hidden behind a pair of red curtains in one of the top windows is the unmistakable glint of a pair of binoculars.

Chapter 9

The Mystery Visitor

Last night, the chimney in my room echoed with bubbles and fizzes until well after midnight.

'Did you hear strange noises coming from next door last night?' I ask Betsy and Mum over our breakfast pancakes.

'No, my gorgeous girl,' says Mum. 'I had my headphones in all night,' she explains. 'I've started to listen to Italian whilst I'm asleep. I read that if you do it every day for a year you can become fluent in a new language without even trying! Isn't that amazing?'

'What did you learn?' I ask her.

'Well not much yet,' Mum admits. 'But it was my first go so maybe I'll pick more up tonight.'

'Betsy?' I ask. 'Did you hear anything?' But she just rolls her eyes at me and goes back to reading her book about teenagers falling in love with each other with a really soppy picture on the front cover.

I need to begin my mission. I take a deck chair from the shed and set it up in the front garden. Then I get myself a pad of paper and rip out all the used pages. I find a pencil that doesn't actually need sharpening and I sit and wait.

***

I've been sitting in my front garden for nearly an hour keeping watch and nothing much has happened. Someone came by asking about a missing rabbit. That reminded me about Kirstyn's rabbit, Nibbles. I'd completely forgotten to tell the others about her so I write *Nibbles* on the first page of my notebook. The postman came to drop off some boring brown envelopes for Mum and a magazine for Betsy. Mrs Tattle came over to say hello and ask what I was doing out in the garden. I didn't tell her of course, I just said it was a nice place to sit and read my book. Then I realised I didn't have a book with me but I don't think Mrs Tattle noticed. She's always poking around and acting very suspiciously so I wrote her name under Nibbles'. Then nothing else of any interest happened.

Catt the dog is lying on my feet and Pyjamas the cat has stretched out on top of the car where he can get the most sun. It's so peaceful and warm that, for a little while, I put my head back and I forget about everything. I forget about the weird things going on and the investigation and I forget about the awfulness that has moved next door.

'Good boy, Frankie,' says a voice that brings me straight back to reality with a mean bump. I look up to see Billy standing on the pavement outside our gate and, through the bars, I can see his dog doing a massive poo right there on the pavement.

'Oi!' I shout without really thinking.

Billy looks at me and waves.

'Nice morning for it,' he says as though we always share chit-chat whilst he lets his dog poop right outside my gate. 'Aren't you going to say thank you to Frankenstein? After all, it's only polite when someone leaves you a little present.'

I can still hear him chuckling to himself as he opens his front door and goes in.

'Didn't you know that Frankenstein was the inventor and he made a pet monster with half a brain. So, if the dog is Frankenstein does that make you the half-brained monster?' I shout after him. Actually, I whisper it quietly to myself but it makes me feel a tiny bit better.

The whole dog poo shoe thing is still fresh in my mind and I know I'll be the one to step in Frankie's *little present* if I leave it lying there so I go inside and get one of Catt's poop scoop bags. This is the only bad thing about having a dog. I HATE picking up the poo. And I'm doubly mad about this one as it's not even my dog's! I turn the bag inside out and put it over my hand. Then I reach down and pick the poop up but, before I turn the bag back the right way to hold the poo, I notice something

47

really weird. The poo looks like it's glowing. I take a closer look inside the little black bag and there's absolutely no doubt that it's most definitely giving off a gentle glow.

'What on earth have they been feeding that dog?' I whisper, wrinkling my nose up and tying the bag to drop it in the wheelie bin. Glowing poo must count as weird enough to go in the notebook but before I have a chance to pick my pencil up again, I notice Catt standing with her nose stuck in the hedge that separates our front garden from the Belchers. Her doggy ears prick and all the fur on the back of her neck stands up straight. She starts a low growl that sounds like the shiny man opposite us when he starts his fancy car with the enormous exhaust pipe. Pyjamas jumps off the car and runs around the back of the house.

'What's the matter, Catt?' I whisper.

As quietly as I can, I move across to the hedge and pretend to be examining it to see if it needs a trim or not, just in case anyone wanders past and wonders why I'm staring at the hedge.

Really though I'm trying to get a good look at what's going on next door. Through the greenery I can see a man wearing a strange green coat and a pair of glasses that are so enormous they might even be goggles. It's the same man I saw shouting at the removal guys and I think it must be Billy's dad, the super scientist. He's standing on the doorstep talking to someone but the other person is completely blocked, partly by the professor and partly by the enormous stack of boxes they seem to be carrying so I can't see who it is. Then the professor steers the person inside and shuts the door.

I feel really cross with myself for not being able to see who the visitor is so I stay by the hedge hoping to a get a glimpse of them on their way out.

I wait for at least five minutes but the person with all the boxes is still inside. Then I hear a van pull up and a Packageforce delivery guy in a pukey-green coloured uniform goes up to the Belchers' front door and rings the bell.

The door opens and an arm comes out, signs the little delivery form, grabs the package and slams the door shut all pretty much in one swift move.

'Hmm, interesting!' I say to Catt, making a note in the investigation book to say what time it is and what I saw.

'What's interesting?' a voice from the other side of the hedge makes me jump.

'Oh, hi Billy,' I say as calmly as I can manage. 'I was just looking at the hedge to see if I should come out later and cut it a bit.

'That's not interesting,' Billy spits back and actually he's right.

'No, what I meant by that was...' I look around to see what could possibly be interesting about the hedge. I see a plain, extremely ordinary ladybird and it gives me an idea. '...there was a huge ladybird. With a green back and purple spots,' I add just to make it even more

interesting.

'Where?' Billy asks from right behind me and I wonder how on earth he could get round to my side of the hedge so quickly.

'Oh, it just flew away,' I tell him, trying to sound sorry but his attention is caught up with something else.

'What're you writing?' he asks and, before I realise what's happening, my investigation notes have been snatched away from me.

'Give that back,' I yell at Billy and try to grab my book. It's no use though because he's much taller than I am and stronger too.

'Let's have a look here,' he says, enjoying making me cross.

'Hey!' he shouts seeing what I have written. 'Are you spying on us?'

'No!' I say. 'Of course not.'

'Why've you written down what's going on at my house then?'

'Um, it's a... er... a homework project.' I give myself a little cheer inside my head to say well done for being such an excellent detective. 'Yes, I have to monitor the people who come and go in our street. Look, it's not just your house, there are other names here too.'

'Who the heck is Nibbles?' Billy asks.

'Oh that?' I say, trying to think on my feet. 'That's what I call my sister Betsy.'

'You call your sister Nibbles?'

'Yes, that's right. It's because she always... um...

she used to... nibble... um... my toes.'

'Your sister used to nibble your toes?' Billy asks, looking bemused.

'Only when I was a baby,' I explain. 'She doesn't do it anymore.'

Luckily for me, Billy seems to be bored of hearing my baby stories.

'I don't remember this homework,' he says suspiciously.

'You never bother with homework though, do you Billy?' I reply.

Billy thinks about that for a little while. It almost looks as though his brain is working extra slow trying to figure out what to say next.

'That's true,' he says.

I think there's a chance I may get away with it. 'Can I have my book back please?' I ask.

''Homework's for suckers,' Billy decides and pulls a little red lighter out of his pocket which makes a tiny flame when he flicks a button.

'What're you doing?' I ask, feeling a bit shaky. I remember Betsy telling me about a boy from her school who set his jumper on fire when he messed about with a box of matches. She said that by the time he got to hospital his arms looked like they were made out of red plastic and they were never right again.

Billy holds the tiny flame under my book.

'No!' I shout but this just makes him grin even wider and I know exactly what he's going to do.

I run in to the house to grab a jug of water. The tap seems to take ages to fill it up. When I get back outside, Billy's gone and my book is in the middle of the pavement with flames bouncing off it. My book isn't the only thing burning and angry. I am red hot mad too at how unfair this all is. I loved living next door to Mr and Mrs Custard and things in my road were great. But now I have to live by the nastiest boy in our school and he thinks he can go around burning my stuff. I don't get mad too often but I'm as furious as the Queen of Fury on a bad day right now.

I chuck the water over the book and the flames hiss out leaving behind them a very soggy, burned mess of blackish paper.

I sit down on the kerb, waiting to make sure it's definitely not going to start burning again like those magic cake candles that start up for a second go just when you think you're safe.

Suddenly something rams into my back, making me squeal. I look around, expecting to see Billy but instead there's a lady wobbling right behind me with a massive sun hat pulled so far down over her dark glasses she can't see where she's going.

'Oh sorry, dear. I didn't see you there,' she says, backing away. Then she trips on the curb and falls backwards on her bottom, dropping her bag on the ground. The glasses fall from her face and I recognise her straight away. It's Cherry McPhizz from the new sweetshop in town. Mum hasn't let me go there yet but her picture has been in the paper a lot and Sid, who has the sweetest tooth of all of us, has a leaflet about the shop stuck on his noticeboard.

'Are you alright Mrs McPhizz?' I ask, going over to see if I can help her out.

'Oh,' she says, scrambling to her feet and shoving the glasses back on her nose. 'I'm fine. Absolutely fine. It's this blasted hat, can't see a thing.'

'It's a lovely hat though,' I say.

She smiles at me. 'Yes, well needs must I'm afraid. I do suffer so terribly in this awfully strong sun. Turn pink as a flamingo as soon as I step outside. And then there's the pollen as well.' She points to her sunglasses. 'Makes my eyes itch you see.'

'Yes,' I agree. 'It must be awful.'

'I am so sorry to knock into you,' Cherry McPhizz says to me. 'Are you hurt?'

'It's alright,' I say, thinking how nice she is to worry about me when she had the worse tumble.

'I was just delivering leaflets about some new offers at the sweet shop,' she says and starts rummaging in her massive red bag.

'Here you are,' she says, offering me a pile of flyers. 'You can also have a little something from me to say sorry for crashing into you.' She gives me another, smaller piece of paper.

I look down at it. It's bright pink with purple and blue swirly writing sandwiched between a picture of a jar of sweets and one of those huge stripy lollies that no-one ever finishes.

MCPHIZZ'S SWEET EMPORIUM
£10 VOUCHER

That will buy me an awful lot of strawberry laces.
'Thank you!' I say, looking up. But Cherry McPhizz is already half way down Howahorse Road, bumping into lamp posts as she goes.

Chapter 10

The Sweet Emporium

Mum says she has to go into town to buy some orange wool for her knit-your-own dog kennel project.

The others would probably tell me to stay behind and carry on with the investigation but I've had enough of sitting in my front garden watching the road. Besides, if I go into town with Mum it means I can buy a new notebook and spend my sweet shop voucher.

We stop first at Farrans, the art shop, and Mum chats to the lady behind the counter about different fibre-tip, felt-tip, brush-tip, fine-liner, thick-liner, medium-liner marker pens that might be useful if she's going to try her hand at illustrating children's books. I roll my eyes and leave her to it whilst I go to the notebook section. I pick several up and turn them over in my hands, testing out how they feel. I can't find any fireproof notebooks, so I opt for one covered in little cartoon pictures of dogs. It has a label on the front for me to write on and the pages have grids of squares which might be useful for drawing maps or plans. It has a matching pen tucked into a little sleeve and an elastic band that keeps everything together. There's even a neat flap at the back for me to put any evidence we might find.

I take the book back to the counter where Mum has moved away from marker pens and is now quizzing the shop assistant about watercolour paint brushes.

'I think I may go for a style a little like Quentin Blake,' she says. 'He's always had a way with paints, hasn't he?'

'Come on, Mum,' I say as I hand over the money for the notebook. 'Why don't you look into illustration once the dog kennel's finished.'

'You're right, my darling. One thing at a time.'

We leave Farrans and walk along the high street to the wool shop at the far end of town.

'That's exactly the colour I was thinking,' Mum says, picking up a disgusting, satsuma-coloured ball of wool. I feel so sorry for Catt. She's not going to know what's hit her when Mum finishes her new kennel and expects Catt to live in it.

'Now I just need to nip to the charity shop, see if they've got any scarves,' Mum says, steering me towards a shop so stuffed with other people's old things that I can almost hear it crying.

'Do you mind if I go to Cherry McPhizz's sweetshop instead?' I ask. 'It's only over there and I can meet you back here when I've finished.'

'Of course, my lovely,' says Mum. 'Just don't buy anything that will make all your teeth fall out before the end of the day.'

I leave Mum to see if she can add any more floaty scarves to her enormous collection and I walk over to Cherry McPhizz's Sweet Emporium.

In the window of the shop is an amazing display of everything sugary. Every colour of the rainbow - and some the rainbow doesn't know exist - fill the display. It reminds me of the field in Charlie and the Chocolate Factory where everything they see is edible and I love it.

It's only been open for a little while and already Cherry McPhizz's Sweet Emporium is the most popular shop in the whole of the town. Well, it is to me all the kids at school anyway!

I walk through the door and it feels like I've just walked into a different land. Nothing bad could ever happen in a sweet shop, especially one as amazing as this.

Inside, the floor is covered in bright swirly patterns and the ceiling is painted to look like the sky on a sunny day with little marshmallowy clouds and a huge sun smiling from one corner. I can't see the walls because they are absolutely covered with shelves. There are loads of jars set out on the shelves so it looks like one of those old-fashioned sweet shops you see in history books and on the telly. I can see round sweets covered in sugar and square ones made from layers of different colours. Huge gobstoppers that I'm sure I couldn't even fit in my mouth, although I might buy one for Betsy. Long worms made from jelly, fizzy crocodiles, fudgey beans, even a life-sized pair of wellies that are made from chocolate.

For a moment, I stand in the middle of the shop and breathe in hard. I'm sure the air tastes of sugar and fruit and cola and everything else that make sweets the perfect food.

'Can I help you?' asks Cherry McPhizz stepping through the door behind the till.

'Hello, Mrs McPhizz,' I say. 'I've come in to use the voucher you gave me this morning.

The shop keeper looks very different from the lady who knocked me over on the pavement. Obviously, she doesn't need the sun-glasses and huge hat inside and they've been replaced by a tiny pair of normal glasses and a neat red bow in her bunned hair. She's wearing a red and white stripy dress and a white apron that looks like it should be on a Victorian doll. Her eyes are all twinkly and her cheeks are rosy pink and dimpled. Nobody could be a better fit as a sweet shop owner.

'Ah yes,' she says and gives me a lovely smile. I wonder if all people who want to own sweetshops have to learn to smile and be nice to children. The lady at the butcher never smiles and the man who works at the baker even makes Mum leave me outside when we go because he says his shop is not the place for children. But Cherry McPhizz looks very pleased to see me in her sweet emporium.

'Have you got any strawberry laces?' I ask her

58

because if I have free money to spend in a sweet shop Daisy would not to talk to me again if I didn't buy some strawberry laces for everyone.

'Of course,' she says and points to one of the jars.

I pull it from the shelf and pass it over the counter.

'How many can I get with my voucher?' I ask.

Cherry McPhizz takes out a huge handful and puts them on a metal tray to weigh them.

'That's just over £3,' she says and I can't believe my luck. 'Do you want more or are you going to mix it up with something else?' she asks.

I decide that I've probably got enough laces so I wander around the shop to choose something else. I go for some jellies in the shape of aliens because I think Sid will like them and some fizzy things that look like stripy goats. I have plenty to share with the others and there is still enough of the voucher left to buy Mum a couple of chunks of chocolate fudge.

'Good choices, young lady,' says Cherry McPhizz and she smiles again. I'm so glad she moved to our town and decided to set up her shop close to us.

I hand over the voucher and she gives me a big bag with all my sweets inside. It feels lovely and bulgy and I can't wait to get back and show the others.

'Thanks, Mrs McPhizz,' I say. 'I'll be back again, when I get my pocket money!'

'And tell your friends to visit me too,' she says. 'I do love visits from children. Here, take one of these for good luck.'

She pushes a basket of little sugar mice towards me. They have string tails and tiny pink noses and look almost too cute to eat.

'Thank you,' I say and choose a yellow mouse deciding that, cute or not, it definitely needs eating.

'See you again,' Cherry McPhizz says and I wave to her on my way out.

I'm just about to walk down to meet Mum when something catches my eye. There, lurking in the doorway of an empty shop on the other side of the road, is a woman with an enormous nose and a woolly hat pulled down over long, curly, brown hair (even though it's really *really* hot out today.) She's pretending to be on her phone, texting or something. But I can tell she's taking photos and I can also tell that those photos are of me.

'Hey!' I say.

She tucks the phone into her bag and marches off down the street. Her disguise was not brilliant to be honest. A rubbish wig and fake nose that looked like it came out of a Halloween costume box is not enough to fool me.

I take out my new notebook. On the first page I write:

Mrs Tattle. Lurking outside school and now the sweet shop. All places kids go. VERY SUSPICIOUS.

Chapter 11

The Alien Invader and O-B-1

That evening Mum calls *family time* and we all sit on the sofa watching old films and eating popcorn. Catt is far too big to be a lap dog but try telling her that. I don't mind though as I love her curling up, half on me and half on the sofa. It's nice having an evening off and I try not to think about any of the weird stuff that's been happening.

I give Mum the chocolate fudge I bought her and I even share some of the other things with Betsy. For a while it's almost back to how things used to be.

But then, when I go to bed, I find I don't sleep well. My mind is full of Mrs Tattle, Billy Belcher, glowing poo and flashing houses.

As soon as I wake up I walkie-talkie Daisy.

'Sunny Daise,' I radio through. 'Come in, Sunny Daise.'

I don't have to wait for long before a crackle

comes through my line.

'This is Sunny Daise. What's news, Mima Bear? Over.'

'Calling a meeting for the whole team at headquarters to discuss developments in the investigation. Over.'

'Roger that, Mima Bear. How urgent?'

'I need my breakfast first. Let's say nine thirty. Over.'

'Right. I'll contact O-B-1. You send a message to Alien Invader. Meet you at nine thirty. I repeat, nine thirty. Over and out.'

After breakfast, I shout through to Mum to tell her I'm off to see Alien Invader. Of course, I don't use his code name, that's the whole point of a code name. It's supposed to be secret. So, I just call him Sid.

Daisy and O-B-1 (AKA Olivia Brown) meet us back at my house.

'I have a new investigation notebook,' I announce as soon as everyone's there. I show them the gorgeous pad I bought in town.

Daisy takes it and looks at the first page.

'Mrs Tattle. Lurking outside school and now the sweet shop. All places kids go. Very suspicious,' she reads out. She flicks through a few more pages and then looks at me.

'There's not much in it Mima,' she says.

'Of course there isn't,' I explain, 'I only got it yesterday.'

'So, what's the point in showing it to us then?' Daisy sounds a bit grumpy. I think it must be because her skin's still covered in green spots. She says it doesn't bother her much anymore but it would bother me I'm sure.

'I thought you'd like to know why I had to get a new book,' I start to explain. I tell the others about the mystery visitor next door and Frankenstein's glowing poo. I wasn't sure they'd believe me about the poo but I suppose, after the flashing house nothing sounds strange anymore.

Then I tell them about how Billy Belcher appeared in my garden and saw what I'd written in my notebook.

'He thought it was my homework,' I say. 'And then he thought it would be fun to set fire to it.'

'He's probably been taken over by aliens,' says Sid and we all groan. 'Seriously, why else would he set fire to your book? And if you think about it, that would explain a lot of his other weird behaviour.'

'It's a shame you didn't get to see who the visitor was Mima,' says Daisy.

'I know,' I say and I feel a bit stupid. I sat in my garden all morning and didn't spot the most important clue of all. I'm sure if Olivia or Daisy had been involved in the stake out, they wouldn't have missed it. Maybe even Sid.

'Never mind that now,' Daisy says. 'We need to find some real evidence about Mrs Tattle, Mr Wrenchitt and Professor Belcher and that means we're going to have to become spies.'

We decide to start with the Belchers.

'We just need to look through the windows to see what's actually going on in the house,' Daisy says. 'But we know Mrs Tattle is keeping watch for them so how are we going to sneak round without her seeing?'

'Don't worry about Mrs Tattle,' Olivia says. 'She has all her bridge crones over at the moment, I saw them arriving when we walked past her house. They'll be there for hours so Mrs Tattle won't be able to watch anyone except the Queen of Hearts.'

'What on earth are bridge crones?' I ask her.

'A bunch of women who go round and play cards, eat sandwiches and drink tea,' Olivia explains. 'She asked my mum to go once and Mum said it wasn't really her thing so she hasn't been again.'

'That's brilliant,' I say. 'But we still have Professor Belcher, Billy and Frankenstein to worry about.'

'I've got a plan,' Sid says. 'We ring the door bell and see if Billy's at home.' Already I don't like the sound of this particular plan, but Sid carries on. 'If he isn't then we can sneak round the back as soon as his dad shuts the front door. It will be easy to keep an eye on just one person and keep out of his sight. Also, if we knock on the door, we'll be able to tell if that crazy dog's home. If it's quiet then it means no Frankenstein.'

'And what if he is there?' I ask.

'Then I'll ask him out for a walk or see if I can get him to come over to my house to play football, pretend

64

I'm welcoming him to Howahorse Road. Leave the way clear for you to go round the back and see what you can find out.'

'You'd have Billy Belcher over just so we can get to snoop around a bit at his place?' I ask. I find it tricky to believe as there is no way AT ALL I would let Billy Belcher come to my house.

'We need to find clues. Right?' asks Sid. I nod and so do the others. 'Well then, asking him round for a game of football is a small price to pay.'

I look at Sid and feel absolutely impressed with his braveness.

'Wow!' I say because I can't think of anything better. I think Sid blushes a tiny bit and he definitely puffs up when he sees how impressed we all are.

'Wait here,' says Daisy as we get up to try out the first stage of the big spy plan. 'I've got something at home that might help us get a better look in without getting caught.

***

As it happens, Billy is not at home when we knock. His dad answers the door wearing the weird green coat which has loads of pockets all over it. His glasses are stuck on the top of his head and he looks a bit cross, probably because we made him stop his mad scientist work to open the door.

'Billy's not here,' Barrington Belcher snaps. 'He's

taken that dog of his to the park on the other side of town to chase pigeons most likely.'

'Do you know when he'll be back?' Sid asks.

'Not for ages so there's no point coming round again today,' says the professor and shuts the door right in our faces.

'He won't be back for ages,' Daisy says, 'so there's nobody watching if we sneak around the back.

'What about Billy's dad?' I ask. I can't believe everyone else has forgotten the really grumpy man who was so cross when we rang his door bell. 'I don't like the thought of him catching us snooping around his garden.'

'He won't be expecting us so, if we're really quiet - stay below the windows and close to the wall, we should be okay,' says Daisy.

'Besides, he's too busy doing weird sciencey, flashing stuff to worry about what's happening outside his window,' adds Sid.

Olivia doesn't look happy.

'Maybe it would be a good idea if one of us waits near the road to keep an eye out for Billy,' she says. 'Just in case.'

We decide that Sid is the best person to keep watch. He's the best at making cat fighting noises to warn us if anyone comes. We did think a bird noise would be the perfect warning signal but nobody can make a good one. We all sound like people trying to make bird noises and doing it badly. I can do a pretty good impression of a howler monkey but that's not very useful where we live. Daisy is excellent at dolphin clicking and Olivia can do Mrs Rees's voice very well. Neither of those are very useful warning alarms either but Sid's cat fight is good enough.

So, the plan is set. Sid stands on the pavement outside where he can see up and down the road as well as Mrs Tattle's house.

'Good luck everyone,' he says bravely. We all take a deep breath and then Olivia, Daisy and I go down the passageway at the side of the Belchers' house.

Chapter 12

Snooping for Clues

We move as quietly as we can and, when we get to the back, we duck down underneath the window so that we can't be seen. We keep very still and listen. The house is humming with strange sounds. The bubbling noises I sometimes hear through the chimney in my bedroom are mixed with a weird buzzing.

When Mr and Mrs Custard lived here, Betsy and I went over for tea as often as we could. Mrs Custard loved baking things and was a brilliant cook but she said it was hardly worth it for just two people. She asked Mum if she could borrow us and we always loved it because it made a nice change from Mum's pineapple and pickled onion omelette. This is now useful because I know the layout of the house almost as well as my own. I know that the window we are crouching under is the kitchen window and the big glass doors next to it lead into the living room. The bubbling sounds are coming from the window which makes sense because to make things bubble you really need a cooker and where else would you find a cooker but in a kitchen?

'We need to see inside,' I whisper. I don't like the idea of poking our heads up because if Professor Belcher is in there, he's bound to see us.

Daisy puts a finger to her lips and pulls something flat out of her pocket. It looks like a couple of mirrors stuck to a piece of cardboard. Then she pops one bit and twists another bit and it turns into a long tube with a bend at the top and the bottom. *Well done Daisy!* I think because it's one of those spy periscopey things that help you look round corners or over the top of something. They put huge ones on submarines so sailors can look above the sea without getting wet or drowning.

Daisy is using hers to have a look through the window. She moves it around a little bit and then watches. It's absolutely brilliant that she was clever enough to think about spy equipment but I wish she had more than one. It's really annoying watching her investigate whilst Olivia and I can only stare at the bricks and the broken patio slabs we're crouching on.

After a few minutes, Daisy passes the periscope to me and I hold it up to the window. Mrs Custard's friendly kitchen is still there but it's now absolutely full of mad inventor stuff. The cooker has two enormous pots on it, both bubbling away furiously. There are also four other little cookers, like the ones people take with them when

they go camping, and each one has a huge pot on it. Some of the pots have tubes sticking out of them which lead to glass jars. Brightly coloured liquids glug along the pipes and it actually looks so pretty I could almost forget that the stuff in there is probably total evil.

Professor Belcher is stirring one of the pots with a long wooden spoon. Then he tucks the spoon into one of the pockets of his green coat and takes a pencil from behind his ear. He scribbles something down in a little purple notebook and then taps some numbers into a calculator. He writes something else in the notebook and then puts the book and the calculator in his coat pocket and tucks the pencil back behind his ear.

Olivia taps me on the shoulder and I pass her the periscope. She looks through for a couple of minutes. Then she turns around and wafts around her nose.

'What?' I mouth to her.

'Can you smell it?' she whispers.

Daisy and I take in huge nosefuls of air and I do smell something. It's sweet and fruity and full of vanilla and other yummy things.

Before she passes the periscope back to Daisy, Olivia shuffles along until she's next to the big glass doors that lead into the living room. She angles the periscope so that she can see inside and watches for a bit. Then it's Daisy's turn and then finally I get to look.

Inside there is a long sofa and a telly but that's where it stops looking like a regular sitting room. I can count another five camping cookers, each one propped

up on bricks. That's five more pots bubbling away. The big fire place at the edge of the room has a strange tripod over it and from that dangles an enormous pot. It's not lit at the moment but I bet it was last week when I heard all the strange bubbling noises coming from our joined up chimney.

Just then, Sid makes the cat fight emergency alarm and I jump and drop the periscope.

I realise that we all decided *how* Sid would warn us of danger, but we didn't plan *what to do* if we heard it!

I look at Daisy and Olivia. Surely one of them must have a good plan. They're much better at plans than I am. But nobody is moving. I know if we stay where we are, we're bound to get caught. Maybe we could make a run for it to the back of the garden and try and push through the hedge where it's not as thick as it is here. That wouldn't work though as it would take ages for all of us to squeeze through. Even if we weren't seen running through the garden, we'd be caught trying to get through the hedge.

I, for one, don't like our chances if we get caught. Professor Belcher is pretty mean and now Billy is back too.

GRRRRRRR GROOF WOOF GRRRR!

The noise at the patio doors makes us jump again. Billy's awful dog is also back and he clearly knows something is up.

'BILLY,' Barrington Belcher shouts from the kitchen. 'Shut that dog of yours up, will you?'

'Sorry Dad.' Billy's voice comes from the living room. 'Quiet, Frankenstein.'

But Frankenstein the dog is not going to stop. If anything, the growling gets more ferocious and the barking gets louder.

'What is it, boy? Is there something out there?'

The three of us flatten ourselves against the wall. I hear the glass door jiggle but nobody comes out.

'I'll get the key, Frankie,' Billy says to the still growling dog. 'If there are any cats out there you can teach them a lesson for trespassing in our garden.'

I'm not a cat but I don't like the thought of being taught a lesson by Billy or his snarling dog if they catch us.

'This way,' I whisper and scuttle back under the kitchen window. I get to the corner of the house and go around to escape up the side alley. Only, just as I do, I bump straight into someone coming the other way.

Chapter 13

The Lost Periscope

'm relieved when I see who I've bumped into.

'Sid!' I say.

I'm so glad to see him that I give him a hug. He looks a bit embarrassed but it's okay because we can't hang around to discuss hugs as it won't take Billy long to get the key and let out his crazy dog.

'The coast is clear,' whispers Sid. 'This way.'

All four of us disappear up the path and get back to my front garden just as the mad dog, Frankenstein, comes charging round the side of the Belchers' house. I shut our gate and the dog barks like crazy at the barrier I've put between us. I can feel my heart thumping hard. I'm sure if the gate wasn't there those sharp fangs would now be stuck in my leg or somewhere even worse.

'You need to keep that dog of yours under control,' Sid says bravely to Billy who comes puffing up

73

behind.

'Who says he isn't under control?' he asks. 'Who says this isn't exactly what I asked him to do?'

I can see Sid getting cross so I pull him away and we all go inside my house. Catt is sitting at the bottom of the stairs, looking at the door and growling softly. She wants us all to know (from a safe distance) that she is *not* impressed by Frankenstein. Pyjamas is curled in a ball halfway up the stairs, not in the tiniest bit worried by all the fuss. I stroke them both on my way past. Pyjamas doesn't move but Catt follows us up to my attic room.

'I think we need something for the nerves,' I say and get out the big bag from McPhizz's Sweet Emporium. I hand round the fizzy stripy goats and we suck one each. Mine tastes of cola and cherries and lemonade and it is gorgeous. My hands have stopped shaking now and I root round for the bag of jelly aliens.

'Jellien anybody?' I say passing the bag to Sid.

'Cool,' he says and takes two before passing it on to Olivia.

'So Red Bullet,' he says in a deep alien voice moving the green jellien around like a candy puppet. 'Did you accomplish your mission?'

'Yes, oh Grand Green Master,' his voice has gone high and squeaky. Now the red jelly is talking. 'I successfully implanted our species into the boy called Billy and the dog they call Frankenstein.'

'Very good,' the green jelly alien master says. 'You are now my official second in command and can help me

74

rule over all the Earth when the invasion is complete.'

I think Sid's quite funny but Daisy and Olivia just ignore him.

'Well there's no doubt now that the Belchers are up to something very suspicious indeed,' says Daisy. 'I'd love to know what he has boiling away in all those pans.'

'What about the notebook?' Olivia says. 'If I could have a good look at just one thing in that house then it would be the notebook. I bet he has details of all his experiments written down in there.'

'And I'm sure it must explain how Mr Wrenchitt and Mrs Tattle are involved,' I add. I just know the dentist and the nosy neighbour are vital to this mystery, I just need to work out how.

'Do you think the stuff you saw boiling in the pots has something to do with Daisy's green spots and Juno's webbed toes as well as all the other weird things?' Sid asks us.

'Of course it does,' Daisy says and we all know she has to be right.

'You'd make a good spy,' I tell Daisy. 'I wouldn't have thought of bringing a periscope.'

Daisy looks really pleased.

'Can I have it back please?' she asks. And then I remember the problem.

'Oops,' I say and I can feel my face getting hot.

'What do you mean *oops*?' Daisy asks

'I dropped it outside the Belchers' house,' I tell her. 'When Frankenstein started barking through the window, I got such a jump and I... well I sort of dropped it.'

'Mima!' The others all look pretty mad.

'It's alright,' I say, trying to make up for my mistake. 'I'll buy you another one with my pocket money. Where did you get it?'

'I made it actually,' says Daisy. 'But that's not the point.'

'Well what is the point?' I ask, feeling a bit cross myself that everyone is making such a big deal about it. 'I'll help you make a new one.'

'Don't you see though?' says Olivia. 'If Billy Belcher or his dad find the periscope they'll know someone has been snooping around.'

'Oh rats.' I say, feeling stupid. 'That is a problem.'

'That's not all,' says Daisy, looking very pale under all the green spots. 'I used mum's old dial-your-own-sticker machine to make a label for it. If they do find it then they'll see exactly who it belongs to. Even Billy could work out who was snooping if there's a name tag on the main clue.'

'Double rats!' I say and I feel awful.

There's nothing for it. I got us into this mess so it's down to me to get us out of it. With a knot the size of a watermelon twisting in my guts I realise what that means. I'm going to have to go back to the Belchers' house and get the periscope.

Chapter 14

Getting the Periscope

It's definitely time to bring out the strawberry laces. Usually when we play the strawberry lace game there's a lot of giggling and lace swinging and everything seems a lot better. Today though we're all a bit worried at the thought of Daisy's name sticker and what will happen when Billy or the professor find it.

Sid's best idea is to make a periscope-grabbing device long enough to lean out of my bedroom window and stretch over to the Belchers' garden. The trouble with this is that, even if we could think of a way to make a grabbing device that would work, we can't see the periscope from my window. We have looked but the place where I dropped it is blocked by a bit of overhanging roof.

'What if we stick something through the hedge and hook it on to the periscope from Mima's side?' Daisy suggests. 'Then we could just pull it through.'

'No good,' says Olivia. 'There's a wooden fence on their side behind the hedge at this end of the garden remember.'

'I think we need some hot chocolate.' I say and leave the others in my room whilst I go downstairs to the kitchen. I don't really want to make everyone hot chocolate, it's just that I need an excuse to go down on my own. I have a plan. It's not a great plan but I know it's completely my fault we lost the periscope so it has to be me who goes round to fetch it.

I can't just go round the back like before because if Billy and Frankenstein hear me, I'm definitely a goner. My plan is so simple it may just work. All I need to do is knock on the door and ask for it back. For this to work I am relying on two things. First, that Billy opens the door not his dad. And second, that Billy is as daft as I think he is.

My heart feels like it's about to fall out of my mouth any moment as I knock on Billy Belcher's front door. As soon as I knock, Frankenstein starts barking from inside the house.

When the door opens and I see Billy and his horrible dog, I begin to think my plan is a pretty rubbish one after all and wish I'd just made the hot chocolate and stayed at home waiting for the others to come up with a better plan.

'Skunk Breath!' Billy sneers at me. 'What do you want?'

I have to pull all the courage from my toes right up

78

through my body as far as my mouth to get it to open. Even then the voice that comes out is very tiny and doesn't sound much like me.

'I just wanted to ask you if I could have my mirrors back please? Well, they're not actually mine, they belong to Daisy but she brought them round to my house to play... nature warriors.' I'm on a roll now and my mouth keeps jabbering away. 'We made them into a special bird taming machine and then I leant out of my bedroom window to hang them outside and I dropped them. Right into your garden. So please could I pop round to pick them up?... ' I tail off. Billy is looking at me as though I am completely mad.

'I don't believe you,' he says and my heart beats even faster, absolutely sure he knows exactly what's going on.

'Nature warriors? That's a load of rubbish,' he says, narrowing his eyes.

I gulp.

'I think you're lying to me,' he says. 'I bet you're really playing a girly princess game and you want to tame the ickle birdy wirdies so you have lots of teeny tiny friends to play with you?'

I breathe out in relief. 'Um, yes. You got me. Fairy Princesses.'

'You're even more of a pea-brain than I thought. What an idiot! It's no wonder you need the birds as your friends. Nobody else would be insane enough to talk to you.'

79

I don't remind him that I have lots of friends, thank you very much. Nor do I point out that people are too scared of him to go anywhere near and so it's Billy who has no friends, not me. Instead I just ask again.

'Could I go and fetch it then?'

'No. You stay here and I'll go and look.' He calls Frankenstein over.

'Come here, Frankie. Good boy. Now you watch her and make sure she doesn't go snooping.'

The dog is even more vicious looking close up. He's the exact opposite of Catt with her long legs and a tail that hardly ever stops wagging. Frankenstein is short and round and his tail sticks out from his bottom in a hard stump. Catt has soft floppy ears and warm brown eyes but Frankenstein's little sharp ears are straight up on his head. His eyes are really small and they look mean as though he would like nothing better than for Billy to give the command to BITE or KILL.

'Good dog,' I say nervously.

GRRRRRRRRRRRRRRRRRRRRR

The growling doesn't stop. It's just one long, constant, throaty noise warning me that if I move even the tiniest muscle, this animal will probably jump at me and sink his teeth in.

And then I see it. On the bottom step of the staircase. Professor Belcher's purple notebook. So close to the open front door I can almost reach in and touch it, but with a growling, sharp-toothed animal between us I'm not stupid enough to try. Frankenstein barks once as though he's read my mind and is reminding me he's there. Like I need reminding! I need him out of the way and I search my brain for an idea. I can only come up with one and I don't like my chances of it succeeding but I have to give it a try because this is a golden opportunity and Billy will be back any moment.

I start to make a buzzing sound like a fly. I know this is the one thing that drives Catt absolutely bonkers and I hope it will work on Frankenstein as well. Instantly he stops growling and his ears swivel forward. He looks agitated and uncomfortable, just like Catt when there's a fly in the room. I keep buzzing until it drives Frankenstein so mad he puts his tail between his legs and bolts out of the front door and down the road.

Without wasting another second, I lean into the house, grab the notebook and stuff it inside my dungarees.

Only just in time as Billy comes back with Daisy's periscope.

'Weird looking bird tamer,' he says, staring at it too closely for my liking.

'It's because we love the little birds so much,' I say, trying to sound pathetic. 'Thank you so much for rescuing our fairy equipment, now we can tame more birds and capture our princess power.'

'Loser,' Billy says but my plan is working. 'Here, take it then if it means so much to you.'

He leans through the door and hands me the periscope. But before I can take it from him, he drops it

on the ground in front of me and stamps on it hard, three times with one foot and then with the other just for good luck.

It's only now he realises something is wrong.

'Hey, where's Frankie?' he asks.

'He saw a cat,' I say and point down the road.

'Stupid cats,' he mutters and starts to follow. Then he turns back and I worry he's about to figure it all out but he reaches past me and pulls the front door of his house shut before disappearing off down the street after Frankenstein.

I pick up the broken bits of glass and the crushed cardboard and I hurry back round to my house. Upstairs the others are still sucking strawberry laces.

'Well,' says Sid when I walk in. 'Where's the hot chocolate?'

Chapter 15

We Need Proof

When I show the others the broken bits of the periscope I expect them to be cross, especially Daisy as it was hers and it's pretty useless now. Instead, she grins an enormous grin and gives me a hug.

'How did you do it?' she asks.

'I just knocked on the door and asked Billy,' I say, secretly pleased by how shocked everyone looks.

'You just asked him?' Olivia says and I nod.

'For a while, I thought he was going to hand it over but then he decided it would be more fun to stamp on it first.'

'I guess that's how it's so smashed up then,' says Daisy. 'But how did you explain why my periscope was in his garden in the first place?'

'It's not a secret spy periscope anymore,' I tell her. 'It's our *fairy princess bird taming enchanter*. Billy

83

thought I was off my nut and he was so busy calling me an idiot that he didn't stop to think what else we could have been using it for.'

'Brilliant thinking, Mima Bear!' says Daisy.

'And that's not all I came home with,' I say proudly and stick my hand inside my dungarees.

'Aw, Mima,' Sid says. 'I'm not sure we want anything that's been lurking in there.'

'I think you might,' I say and pull out the purple notebook.

'That's not...' Olivia says, staring at the book in amazement.

'If you mean Professor Belcher's experimenting notebook, then I can confirm that is exactly what it is,' I say.

'How on earth did you get that?' Daisy asks.

So, I tell them about seeing the book, fly-tricking Frankenstein and watching Billy run off down the road.

'Brilliant,' laughs Sid. 'I wish I'd seen that.'

'Let's have a look then,' he asks and I throw him the book. He opens it up and runs his finger down the first page.

'Hmmm,' he says. 'Interesting.'

'What?' I ask.

'I have absolutely no idea what it says.'

'Give it here,' Daisy says and Sid passes it to her. She looks at the first few pages and then flings it on the floor in frustration.

'It's all nonsense,' she groans.

I pick up the book and take a look for myself. On the first page is a list of letters and next to the letters there are tallies. Some of them have been ticked and some have been left blank. On the following page there are more letters set out in pairs but this time next to each one is a single word. There seems no logic or pattern to the letters or the words. Things like *tennis, cub, Martins, clothes, aliens.*

On the next page is another list of numbers with some sort of code next to them. A mixture of Bs, Gs, Os and more numbers.

I can't begin to see anything that makes any sense so I pass it on to Olivia.

'Time for some more strawberry lace thinking,' says Sid and I hand out another round.

We suck laces, and take turns to stare at the jumble of letters and numbers with no luck until the bag of laces is completely empty. The jelliens have all gone too and there are only a few fizzy goats left when Daisy suddenly jumps up and grabs the book back from Sid.

'They're initials!' she says, jabbing her finger at the page. 'They have to be, that's why they're in pairs.'

She looks hard at the page. 'SP - Siddharth Prasadem. OB - Olivia Brown. DS - Daisy Sparkes. And there you are, Mima - MM.'

We look at all the other letters and can find lots that match the initials of kids in our class. By each one is a word. I am *dogs,* Daisy is *book,* Olivia is *pool,* and Sid is *aliens,* which he seems quite pleased with. But I don't like the thought of Professor Belcher having a list of all our names and I can't imagine what the words next to them mean. Is it a list of clues as to our own personal fates? If so, how are Daisy's spots linked to a book and what on earth does 'dogs' mean for me?

'We should take this to the police,' Olivia says. 'They need to know what the Belchers are up to.'

'We can't,' I say. 'How can we tell them what the Belchers are up to when we don't really know for sure ourselves?'

'Mima's right,' says Daisy. 'We're just kids so why would they listen to us? Everyone has a theory about what's going on and the police can't chase all of them up. They're bound to start with the clues that people like doctors and teachers and the lollipop lady give them. Important people... grown up people. Not a bunch of school kids.'

'So, let's get more proof then,' says Sid. 'Or at least figure out what the clues we *have* got mean.'

We make a list of detective jobs in my notebook.

Go and visit Mr Wrenchitt.

Work on figuring out the coded notebook.

Go to tea at Mrs Tattle's for a snoop around.

Watch the Belchers closely. Very closely.

Buy more strawberry laces.

When everyone else has gone home, I lie on my bed and open the purple notebook. What does it all mean? I stare at the numbers and letters until they start to dance around on the page and my head aches. I reach for the bag of sweets but there aren't any left. Then I remember the little sugar mouse that I'd put in my sock drawer for safe keeping. Not really as good thinking food as strawberry laces but I suppose it will have to do.

I can't find any answers so I give up. It's not all that late but I put my PJs on and brush all the sugar from my teeth.

It's been a very busy day and my bed feels so friendly and comfortable. I can't help closing my eyes.

At some point Mum comes into my room to ask if I want any curried beetroot and pea soup. I'm too tired to eat and anyway it sounds revolting so I tell her I'm not hungry and pull the duvet over my head.

***

I don't open my eyes again until the next morning and I wake up feeling fresh and happy. Then I remember the big problem that's brewing next door, the list of initials, the huge bubbling pots and all the other crazy stuff that's happening at the moment. I also remember that it's Monday and I have to get up for school.

I hunt around for my dressing gown but I can't see it so I put on a fleece instead and wander downstairs to get some breakfast.

Mum is stirring a saucepan and doesn't look round when I come in.

'Morning, love,' she calls over her shoulder. 'Fancy some banana and honey porridge?'

That actually sounds really nice.

'Yes please Mum,' I say and go to the drawer to get some spoons out.

'With Marmite or without?'

'Definitely without, thanks.'

'What on earth have you got sticking out of your pyjamas?' Betsy says, walking into the kitchen.

'Nothing,' I say looking down at my legs.

'Not there, you plum,' she says. 'There!'

She comes up behind me and I feel a sharp tug somewhere just above my bottom.

'Ow!' I say. 'Leave off, Betsy, that really hurt!'

'Now, now, girls,' says Mum. 'Let's all have a bit of porridge and start the morning as we mean to go on.'

She turns around with the big saucepan and then screams loudly and drops the whole thing on the floor.

'Mima!' she says, staring at my bum. 'You've got a tail!'

Chapter 16

Me and My Tail

I put one hand behind my back and feel around. My hand finds a long furry thing and, when I give it a gentle tug, it feels stuck on pretty tight. I can feel it when I give it a tickle, and when I pinch the end and when I try to pull it off. That last one REALLY hurts.

I feel sick. This thing is actually a part of me. I'm a girl with a tail and that can mean only one thing... I am now on the KAW list. My mind flicks back to the purple notebook. *MM dogs.* Is this what Barrington Belcher had lined up for me all along?

'That is the funniest thing I have ever seen!' says Betsy and I shoot her one of my best evil stares.

Mum doesn't think it's so funny and nor do I. She tries hard to make me feel better about it.

'Don't worry, I'm sure nobody else will notice.'

'Of course they'll notice!' I yell at her. 'How many people have you ever seen with a massive tail sticking out of their bum?'

'Well, darling, nobody other than you,' she admits. 'But in that case, you should wear it proudly. Enjoy being one-of-a-kind!'

'I am not *wearing* this,' I say crossly. 'It's growing on me. It's not as though it's my choice and I can just take it off and hang it on a peg when I've had enough. It's not one of your crazy scarves or bonkers dresses. This thing is stuck on and it's not going anywhere.'

'No,' she says. 'I suppose not. Still, if you did have to grow a tail, at least it's a really handsome one. Any dog would be proud to have a super tail like that!'

'MUM!' I yell.

'No, you're absolutely right,' she says. 'This is very serious. I'll cancel my jive-yoga class this morning and we'll go and see the doctor. Find out what can be done.'

I leave her to call the doctors' surgery and I run upstairs to make a more important appointment of my own.

'Sunny Daise,' I shout into my walkie talkie. 'Are you there? Over.'

'I read you, Mima Bear. What's the matter? Over.'

'Cheese and ham toastie... I repeat, CHEESE AND HAM TOASTIE!' I can't stop my voice from shaking and I even forget to say 'over' so Daisy knows it's her turn. It doesn't matter because she realises it must be important.

'Purple Turtle immediately,' she says. 'Over and out.'

When Daisy sees my tail, she actually looks a little

bit relieved.

'I thought it might be worse,' she says, which makes me even madder.

'How could it be worse than a tail?' I ask her.

She points to her face, still covered in green spots. 'At least you can tuck it into your skirt and people might not notice,' she says which I suppose is true.

'The more important thing to work out is how you ended up with a tail in the first place.'

'Well I didn't go to see Mr Wrenchitt,' I tell her, 'so it can't be that.'

'What did you do?' Daisy asks. 'After we all left you yesterday?'

I tried to think.

'Nothing really,' I say. 'I sat in my room for a bit trying to figure the codes in the notebook out and then I felt really tired so I went to sleep. It wasn't until I woke up this morning that I noticed the tail.'

'What about when you went round to the Belchers' house to get the periscope back?' Daisy suggests. 'Did you touch anything?'

'No,' I said, thinking about Frankenstein keeping me prisoner on the door-step. 'Well except for the notebook, but we all touched that. Lots of times.'

'Well I'm already weird,' she points to her spots again and I shrug my shoulders. 'But maybe the others are waking up as KAWs too?'

I think about that. Would it be better or worse if Sid and Olivia also had strange stuff going on?

91

'What about visitors? Did anyone else come round to your house after we left?'

'No,' I say again. 'Nobody.'

'There must be something,' says Daisy. 'Think, Mima.'

I do think. But there is nothing. I followed all the rules. I hadn't done anything careless or stupid but something still went wrong anyway.

'I just fell asleep and woke up with a tail.'

There is nothing for it but to write down the new information in my investigation notebook and get ready to see the doctor.

I try tucking the tail into my skirt but it sticks out at the back making me look like I'm trying to smuggle a cucumber. I try and hook it over the waistband but it makes my skirt fall down so I have no choice but to take the kitchen scissors and cut a tail hole in my skirt. If I pull my cardigan down then most of it is hidden.

'Nice tail,' laughs a nasty voice as I go outside to wait for Mum by the car.

'Wag your tail for me doggy woggy,' Billy shouts and then ducks away when he sees Mum coming.

'Have you grown a tail dear?' asks Mrs Tattle, appearing from the other side of the road. 'I can't keep up with you young people and your trends.'

I see her binoculars peeking out from under her coat and I stare at her face to see if there's any sign she was expecting to see me with a tail this morning or even that she's pleased to see me as a KAW. But her face is set in a completely neutral smile.

Mum is a messy bundle of bags, coat, several scarves and goodness knows what else. I open the car door for her and she dumps the entire pile on the back seat. We set off and, as we pass the end of the road, I see Daisy walking to school with Sid and Olivia. Mum slows down and I open the window.

'Morning,' I say. 'Are you all alright?' I try and wiggle my eyebrows and open my eyes wide to show them that this is code for *anyone else wake up as a KAW this morning?* But they don't seem to get it.

'What's wrong with your eyes?' Sid asks.

'Oh, nothing's the matter with me,' I say.

'Mima, these are you friends. Don't be shy,' Mum says. 'Hop out and show them your wonderful new tail.'

'Muuuum!' I say, suddenly thinking that it would be a much better idea to wind the window back up and deal with the tail-meet-friends thing later.

'Go on,' she insists, leaning across me and opening the door. Daisy throws me a sympathetic look and I guess she hasn't quite got around to telling them about the tail yet.

'Have a good look,' I say. 'No, I don't know how I got it. Yes, I have tried to think of anything weird that happened after you left last night but no, I didn't come up with anything,' I say snappily, although I know it's not their fault.

'Oh Mima!' says Olivia.

'I like it,' says Sid. 'I think it makes you look like an

animorpher.'

'A what?' I say.

'Someone who can morph into an animal when they feel like it. They always have other secret powers too and can usually save the world in an emergency if they need to.'

I wasn't so sure everyone would see things like Sid did.

'But you're both okay?' I say. There are no obvious KAW symptoms but I just want to double-check.

'Yep, everything fine here,' says Olivia.

'And I can report everything is A-OK on Planet Sid.'

'Honey, I'm afraid we're going to have to get going. We don't want to be late for your appointment, do we?'

There's no point reminding her that she was the one who insisted I get out and show the others my tail in the first place. I just get back in the car, wave to my friends and head off to the doctors.

***

'Well this is a new one for me,' Dr Numperty chuckles as I walk in and he catches sight of my tail. I think he could show a bit more care for his patient but clearly not. 'Bet you've got an interesting *tale* to tell me hey... eh!' he says with a big grin on his face and I look to Mum for support.

'I mean you can't be feeling too *wagnificent* at the moment,' he carries on.

Mum and I sit down in the seats next to his desk and I try to tuck the tail out of sight.

'No need to put your tail between your legs,' he says. 'If you're a good girl today, I might give you a doggy treat before you go.'

'Dr Numperty,' Mum says. 'You have obviously spotted the reason for our visit today and I want to applaud your superior medical talent. However, as a stand-up comedian you are seriously lacking so my daughter and I would both appreciate it if the rather weak jokes could stop now. Perhaps you could get on with what we are hoping you are somewhat better at. Sorting out this little problem.'

The doctor's grin freezes on his face and I squeeze Mum's hand gratefully. When it counts, my mum's the best!

He examines the tail and tests to see how much feeling I have in it. Turns out from root to tip is full of nerves. It is well and truly connected. Luckily, I have never been worried about needles because he has to fill three little bottles with blood from my arm.

'I'll get these sent off to the emergency team at the lab,' he says. 'We should get the results in about 48 hours.'

'What about school?' Mum asks.

'There is no reason why Jemima needs to stay off school. The research so far has shown that these abnormalities are not in any way contagious so she poses no threat to the other children in her class. We are advising all children to be vigilant and monitor their symptoms. If they should change or worsen then you need to come back and see me.'

    'Worsen!' I say. 'How can a tail get any worse?'

Chapter 17

PC Blinkered and PC Cuffer

Mum comes in to school with me and explains to Mr McLachlan in the office why I'm late.

'Oh dear,' he says with genuine concern on his face. He clasps his hands together and peers over his blue-framed glasses at me. 'This is all so very worrying. Where will it end?' he asks. He begins twisting his hands as though he's trying to tie them in knots. His eyebrows are also trying to knit themselves together by the look of it, anyone would think it was him who had woken up with a tail that morning.

'Dr Numperty says there's no reason Mima can't be in school but we need to keep an eye on her to make sure no other symptoms start to show themselves.'

'Don't you worry, dear,' says Mr McLachlan. 'We will take very good care of her. We're expecting the police any moment. They want to have a word with all the children who have recently,' he looks at me and then at my tail, '...well, you know.'

'I do,' says Mum.

'With poor Jemima here, that makes four new cases just this weekend.'

I know one of them is Daisy because this is her first day back at school since her spots appeared. I wonder who the other two are.

'Miss Barker will want to see you,' says Mr McLachlan. 'The others are already in with her, so I'll take you to join them.'

I say goodbye to Mum and follow Mr McLachlan to the head teacher's office.

'Good morning,' she shouts through the door when we knock. 'Come in.'

'I've got another here,' Mr McLachlan tells her and gently pushes me into Miss Barker's office. 'Good luck, dear,' he says and gently dabs the corner of his eye with a little hanky.

Daisy's there, with Izzy Shepherd from Year 3 and Ryan Hardy from Year 6. Izzy has a rather impressive bushy beard but I can't tell what's wrong with Ryan yet.

'Oh dear,' Miss Barker says. 'What happened to you?

I pull my tail round from behind me and shrug. Ryan's eyes almost pop out of his head but I can't tell what Izzy is thinking because most of her face is hidden behind the mask of hair.

The buzzer on the desk buzzes and Miss Barker presses a button.

'Yes, Mr McLachlan?' she says into the little microphone.

'I have a PC Blinkered and a PC Cuffer here to see you,' says Mr McLachlan through the speaker.

'Splendid, show them in.'

Two police officers walk into the room. PC Cuffer shakes hands with Miss Barker, smiles at us and opens her mouth to say something but PC Blinkered doesn't give her a chance.

'Ah, yes I see. Green spots. Lots of them, ' he says, looking at Daisy. 'Make a note, Cuffer.'

PC Cuffer doesn't look very happy to be bossed around but she takes out a tiny notebook and writes down a couple of things.

'Thank you for coming,' Miss Barker says and holds out a hand for PC Blinkered to shake.

The policeman either doesn't notice or just ignores it. His hairy eyebrows move really close together like caterpillars meeting for a chat. Underneath them, his eyes scrunch up and he pulls a really weird shape with his mouth.

'Hmm, a tail,' he says. 'How interesting. Write that down Cuffer. And a rather hairy face on this one.' He then looks at Ryan and rubs his chin as though trying to figure out why he's there.

'And you?' PC Blinkered asks him. 'What has happened to you?'

'I went shopping on Saturday and then I can't remember a chunk of stuff before I woke up in the park

under a bench. I only disappeared for about half an hour I think.'

'Not that,' says PC Blinkered crossly. 'I mean how are you different now?'

'Oh, I see,' says Ryan. 'I don't think I really want to say in front of everyone.'

Ryan seems to be going a bit red. All the children in the office look weird. We've all got something wrong with us so I'm not sure why Ryan has to be the one to go shy.

'Uh, hm,' interrupts Miss Barker. 'If I may officer, I have a note from his mother and it's a rather delicate matter. Perhaps you could just take a look at that?' She tries to show him the note but he just bats it away.

'Don't be silly,' says PC Blinkered and Miss Barker looks pretty annoyed with him.

'Well, sonny, what's the problem?'

Ryan looks really uncomfortable and starts shifting from one foot to the other.

'It's, well, it's just that...' He mutters something quickly and quietly so I can't make it out. Neither can the policeman.

'Speak up!' he says and Ryan takes a deep breath.

'I said that every time I go for a pee it comes out bright green and makes a noise like a trombone,' he tells us, going REALLY red now. I feel bad for him. That's maybe the worst one yet I think. I'd definitely rather have my tail or Daisy's spots or even Luke's beard.

'Right, yes. Green, trumpeting pee, I see,' says PC

100

Blinkered. 'Write it down, Cuffer.'

'Not really trumpeting,' Miss Barker tries to explain helpfully. 'More like a trombone I gather...' she tails off as she realises PC Blinkered is not listening.

'That's all we need for now,' he says, going towards the office door.

'Don't you want to ask the children anything else?' asks Miss Barker.

'Not really,' says the policeman. 'They don't often have anything useful to say.'

Daisy gives me an *I-told-you-so* sort of look and we don't say anything about our investigation or the things we've discovered so far. If we're going to talk to the police about this then we need proper hard evidence and plenty of it.

Chapter 18

A Visit to Mr Wrenchitt

I worry that everyone is going to tease me about my tail but nobody seems all that interested in it. Part of that might be because the kids in our school are getting used to seeing weird things going on, but it's also because everyone is talking about something else awful that happened over the weekend: Margaret De Belvoir Bouffant Burgh has escaped. Jean-Charles, the caretaker, went in on Saturday and fed her but, when Mrs Clarke opened up the library this morning, she had gone! The cage door was open so Jean-Charles mustn't have shut it properly. Some of the girls have decided to make a book of remembrance but I'm not going to write my message in it until I know for sure Mags is not coming back. I have to say I don't like her chances if she's gone outside with all the birds of prey and cats around here. But I have to hope she's just exploring the school a bit and will go back to her cage when she gets hungry.

At break time, Daisy, Olivia, Sid and me all go to the stinky corner of the playground to discuss the new things Daisy and I found out in Miss Barker's office.

Olivia hands out the tissues and we plug our noses.

'It's so sad about Mags,' Olivia says and Sid suggests we hold a three minute silence just in case she was taken by a red kite. Sid can never stay quiet for long so after a minute he says we've probably remembered her enough for now and we should get on with the investigation.

'On our way out of Miss Barker's office, I asked Izzy and Ryan if either of them have been to the dentist lately,' I say. 'Izzy hasn't but Ryan went on Friday after school.'

'I'm not sure how Mr Wrenchitt is involved,' Daisy says. 'But this is not a coincidence.'

'We need to break into his surgery and find out what's going on,' says Sid.

'And you think that'll be easy?' I say. 'What do you suggest? Smash a window or bash the door down?'

'I haven't got the finer points of the plan together yet,' Sid says, looking a bit stroppy.

'He's right though,' Daisy says and I don't know who's more surprised, me or Sid.

'We do need to investigate his surgery,' she continues and Sid gives me an *I-told-you-so* smirk. 'But there's no way we're breaking in. It's far too risky,' Daisy concludes. I give Sid a *not-quite-so-clever-are-you*

eyebrow raise.

'What are you thinking?' Olivia asks.

'Well I was just thinking about when Mima went round to Billy's house and just asked him outright for the periscope back,' Daisy says.

Whilst I really don't mind everyone being reminded of my braveness, I'm not sure what this has to do with breaking into Mr Wrenchitt's surgery.

'It made me think that sometimes the best way not to get caught doing something you shouldn't be doing is to be bold and obvious rather than secretive and sneaky. I mean we can't be caught snooping if we have a proper reason to be there in the first place, can we?' she explains.

'You mean we all get dentist appointments after school?' I say.

'Not exactly,' Daisy says. 'We wouldn't be able to anyway, Mum has to book months ahead to get an after-school appointment.'

'But we could go there for a different reason,' Olivia joins in. 'Like perhaps a school project?'

'Perfect idea,' Daisy agrees. 'We tell them we're doing some research on the health services in our area and ask if Mr Wrenchitt has ten minutes to answer our questions.'

'We can ask him for a tour of the surgery and see if there's anything there that looks suspicious,' adds Olivia.

I'm not sure how successful we'll be, but we

decide to drop in after school and see what we can discover.

The door to the dentist tinkles when we walk in and a lady behind the reception desk looks up and gives us a really friendly smile. She looks very familiar but I can't work out where I've seen her before. She's wearing a name badge that tells us she's called Miss F Philer.

'Hello there, how can I help you today?' Miss Philer says in a sing-song voice.

'We're doing a project at school about health care in our area and we wondered if we could have a chat with Mr Wrenchitt,' Daisy asks.

'That does sound like a good project and very interesting too but I'm afraid Mr Wrenchitt is on holiday at the moment with his mother.'

'On holiday?' Daisy asks.

'Mother?' Sid says in surprise.

'Yes, they've gone to Switzerland for a fortnight but I'm sure he'd be happy to talk to you when he returns. Why don't you pop back then? He'll be back at work after the weekend.'

'So, he hasn't been here for over a week?' Olivia asks and I can see what she's thinking. If he hasn't been here, does this mean he can't be guilty?

'Can we look around his surgery?' I ask.

'I'm afraid Miss Brace, our stand-in dentist, is in there at the moment with a patient.'

We must look pretty disappointed because Miss Philer looks at the computer screen and then back to us.

'You could be in luck,' she says. 'There's been a cancellation so she might be able to have a chat or show you around when her patient is ready to leave.'

'That would be brilliant,' says Daisy. 'Thank you.'

We sit on the comfy seats in the waiting room and I can see Sid eyeing up a bowl of sugar-free sweets on the counter.

'Can we have one?' he asks but Miss Philer shakes her head.

'I'm so sorry, but those are only for children who've been really brave in the dentist chair.' She reaches into a box behind the counter and takes out four trial sized tubes of toothpaste. 'But you can have these and a fresh white and healthy smile instead.'

***

Miss Brace is really lovely. She shows us all the instruments she pokes around mouths with and we all get to look at each other's back teeth with the tiny mirror. We take it in turns to sit in the chair and be tilted backwards and forwards. I see the others sneakily looking around for clues and I do the same. But there's nothing much to notice except for all the dentisty stuff.

'Anyone want a swill of mouth wash?' Miss Brace asks us.

Sid is never one to say no to anything so he swills his mouth out with the bright pink liquid and spits it down the miniature metal sink.

'Eurgghh!' he says, pulling a face like he's sucked a lemon. 'That stuff's gross!'

'Anyone else?' asks Miss Brace.

Daisy, Olivia and I all shake our heads.

'I'll have theirs,' says Sid.

Like I said, he just can't say no.

I have one last quick scout round whilst Miss Brace is busy with Sid and the pink mouth wash. I spot a little photo in a frame sitting on the desk next to the computer. Mr Wrenchitt and an oldish lady are wearing floppy sun hats and smiling out of the photo. He looks different without the dentist mask, hat and funny pyjama clothes he wears to work. He's got a massive smile and crinkly eyes and he actually looks really kind. This makes me scrunch my face a bit whilst I think about what this means.

'I'm really sorry but my next patient is here,' Miss Brace says. 'I hope that was useful for your project?'

'Very useful, thank you,' we say and we leave the room.

On the way out, Miss Philer hands Sid a sugar free sweet from the bowl. 'Maybe just the one,' she says and I swear she gives him a wink.

'She liked you,' I say to Sid as we walk back to Howahorse Road. 'None of us got one.'

'What can I say,' says Sid, unwrapping it and waving it under my nose. 'Nobody can resist the Sidster!'

But, just then, he stumbles on a loose bit of pavement and puts his hand out to stop himself from

diving flat on his face. The sweet falls from his hand and lands on the pavement.

'Three second rule,' he says, quickly picking the sweet up and dusting it off.

'Which is illegal these days,' I remind him and we march him to the closest bin and make him drop the sweet inside.

For the rest of the walk home, we discuss the new evidence. Which basically means we try and work out if we can still link Mr Wrenchitt to the KAWs. To start with he hasn't even been there for the past week.

'But Ryan said he saw him on Friday,' Sid reminds us.

'No, he didn't,' I say. 'He just said he'd been to see the dentist. I assumed he was talking about Mr Wrenchitt but he must have meant a different dentist, maybe Miss Brace.'

'So, is he off our suspect list?' Olivia asks.

'I think he's still on the list,' Daisy says. 'Just much further down.'

'What about that picture of him with his mum?' I say. 'He looked so friendly and happy.'

'Never judge a dentist by his smile,' says Sid.

Things make even less sense now than they did before we went to the dentist's surgery. I need to get home and put it all in the investigation notebook. I also want to look through the professor's notes again and see if I can spot something I've missed so far.

I don't have a chance to look at the book though

because Mum and Betsy are waiting for me with worried faces when I get through the door.

Chapter 19

What Has Happened to Catt?

B etsy doesn't say anything mean to me at all which is very weird. Something is definitely wrong.

'What's the matter?' I ask.

'It's probably nothing to worry about,' Mum says but she's twisting her scarf around her fingers and it looks as though she's trying not to cry.

'Catt is missing,' says Betsy, looking furious but also trying not to cry.

'What do you mean missing?' I ask, beginning to feel a bit sick.

'Missing,' snaps Betsy. 'You know, like not here. Gone. Disappeared.'

'Have you looked in my room?' I say because if she's not in her bed, and I can see that's empty, the beanbag on my floor is her second favourite place to curl up.

'Of course we did,' says Betsy, as though I'm the

biggest idiot on the planet.

'What about the garden?' I suggest. 'She loves sitting under the plum tree when it's sunny.'

'Don't you think we've tried that?' Betsy sounds really cross.

'Oh sweetheart, we've looked everywhere for her,' says Mum, letting the tears go. 'She never wanders off, it's just not like her.'

I go to give her a hug and find that I start crying too.

'Well you two can just stay here and blub and hope she comes back all on her own, ' storms Betsy. 'But I'm going out to look for our dog.'

She grabs her shoes and stuffs them on her feet.

'Why don't you go up Trickor Street and knock on doors,' Mum tells her. 'See if anyone that way has seen her.'

'I think I'll go too,' I say.

'No, Mima, you stay here,' says Mum.

'But I want to go and look for her,' I argue.

'Of course you do my lovely,' Mum sighs. 'Okay, why don't you stick to Howahorse Road? Stay close in case anyone brings her home. I'll go this way and walk down Lowis Lane and back via Boat Road. We'll meet back here later.

Mum and Betsy head off on their own missions and I see Mum stop to talk to Mrs Tattle who's out in her front garden.

'I'm sorry, love, but I haven't seen her,' she says

and I'm sure she's lying. How can anyone as nosy as her not have seen where our dog went?

Then I see the evil, awful, horrible Frankenstein and his equally revolting owner.

'It's a bit early for your evening walk, isn't it, Billy?' Mrs Tattle calls to him.

'Hello Mrs Tattle,' says Billy and it's the first time I've ever heard him be almost polite to anyone.

'You usually go out at seven o'clock sharp, don't you?'

'That's right. Just had to nip out to get Dad the newspapers. I'll be taking Frankie out for his proper walk later.'

'I see you and that lovely dog of yours walk past my curtains at the same time every day,' says Mrs Tattle and I wonder how anyone can describe the thick lump of teeth and muscle as *that lovely dog.*

'That's how I know it's time for me to sit down for a bit with a cuppa, close my eyes and listen to my favourite radio show, *The Marchwells.*'

'Yeah, my dad listens to that too but I hate it so I take Frankie for his walk when it's on,' Billy tells us. 'I don't even know why he listens to it. It always makes him fall asleep and when I get back, he's snoring like an elephant on the sofa.'

'You haven't seen the Malone's dog, have you?' the nosy neighbour calls across.

'No, Mrs Tattle but I'll be sure to look out for it.'

It's like watching a completely different person.

112

And this new side of Billy makes me feel a bit nervous.

'There you go, love,' Mrs Tattle says. 'With the whole neighbourhood on the lookout you'll find her in no time.'

She goes back into her own house and Mum carries on down the street on her search. I try to walk past without having to talk to Billy but he's on my heels and I can feel that dog of his breathing on my ankles.

'So you lost your dog, did you?' he asks.

'She'll turn up,' I say and carry on walking. I wait for Billy's come-back. He's bound to make a joke or tease me about why any dog would want to come back to live with someone as useless as me.

But he doesn't. He looks at the ground and shuffles from one foot to the other. He looks shifty. REALLY shifty. Then he scratches Frankenstein behind his ears.

'I hope you get her back,' he mumbles. And then he's gone, leaving me standing on the pavement staring after him with my mouth open.

Chapter 20

We Need A Rescue Mission

I think of my lovely Catt. I imagine her friendly, brown eyes, her blanket-soft fur and her crazy long tail and I feel a kind of desperation bubble inside me. I need help.

'Sunny Daise... I repeat Sunny Daise... over.'

'I hear you Mima Bear,' says Daisy. 'Over.'

'I have a ham and cheese toastie emergency,' I say. 'With extra ham and cheese.'

'Purple Turtle, two minutes.' Daisy says. 'Over and out.'

'Mum just told me about Catt,' Daisy pants as she crashes through the little plastic door.

'I think Billy knows something about Catt,' I tell Daisy.

'How come?' she asks.

I tell Daisy about the weird meeting with Billy and how shifty he looked when he found out Catt was missing. 'Remember Frankenstein's glowing poo?' I remind her. 'What if there's a link?'

'Do you think she might be round at the Belchers?' Daisy asks.

'I'm not sure but I can't think where else she would have gone. She NEVER goes off on her own,' I say. 'Daise, I'm really worried.'

'We need to go round and, if she's there, we need to get her back,' says Daisy and I give her a big hug. She always knows what to do and, with her at my side, I already feel braver.

'We should go at seven o'clock,' I tell her.

She looks at her watch. 'That's in half an hour. Why then?'

'Mrs Tattle told me that Billy always goes out to take Frankenstein for his walk at seven o'clock,' I explain. 'It's always then because his dad listens to some show on the radio and Billy hates it.'

'So at seven o'clock Billy and Frankenstein will be out of the way,' says Daisy.

'AND Professor Belcher will be listening to the radio. Billy said he usually falls asleep when he listens to his programme so that's the best time for us to go in and look for Catt.'

'We'll need to get past Mrs Tattle's binoculars,' Daisy says but I realise that this is also sorted.

'That's the thing,' I say. 'She listens to the same programme. She says it's her chance to sit down with a cup of tea and shut her eyes for bit.'

'Brilliant plan, Mima Bear,' Daisy says and we start to get things ready for the most dangerous mission of our investigation so far.

Chapter 21

Back to the Belchers

As it starts to get close to seven, Daisy and I go into the spare bedroom. It's at the front of the house and has a perfect view of the road. We pull the curtains across so we can't be seen ourselves but we can keep an eye on the road if we peek out of the edges. It's exactly seven o'clock on the dot when Billy comes out of his house with Frankenstein on the lead, just like Mrs Tattle said. We watch them walk down to the end of the road and turn left onto Lowis Lane.

'It's about fifteen minutes to the common from here,' I whisper.

'Why are you whispering?' asks Daisy.

'I don't know,' I say, still whispering.

'It's good practise,' Daisy says, also whispering now. 'We don't want to make any noise when we go next door.'

I think about Billy walking up to the common and

back and it makes me think of all the times I've taken Catt there. Even if this doesn't exactly give me more courage, it does cement the reason for the mad mission Daisy and I are about to set out on.

'I reckon we've got about an hour at the most,' I work out. 'Fifteen minutes there, half an hour to do a loop of the common and fifteen minutes back again.'

'But we need to try and be out before the end of 'The Marchwells' because that's what's going to keep the professor and Mrs Tattle out of our hair. So that's half an hour really,' Daisy points out.

'Right,' I say. 'We'd better get going then.'

We go carefully around the side of the Belchers' house and into their back garden. Everything is quiet so we creep under the kitchen window and I curse Billy for breaking the periscope because there's no way of checking through the patio doors without being in full sight of anyone inside.

We don't have masses of time so there's nothing for it. I take a deep breath and poke my head round so that I can see in through the glass doors. The camping stoves are now switched off and piled up in one corner and next to them is a pile of cardboard boxes.

I can hear the radio blaring out with a man and woman arguing about some quiz at the village hall.

'What I can't understand though, Jessica, is why you had to bring Ranjeet to the annual village pizza and quiz night when I am supposed to be your

husband.'

'Oh, so now you've remembered you're my husband, have you? It's a shame that didn't cross your mind when you went to Majorca with that floozie from your office.'

'How many times do we have to go through this? Petronella and I were on a research project!'

It sounds really boring and I'm not at all surprised Billy doesn't hang around to listen to this rubbish.

Lying on an old green sofa at the far end of the room is a man. I can't see his face because it's hidden under an open copy of a magazine. But there's only one person it can possibly be.

'He's in there,' I mouth to Daisy.

'Is he asleep?' she mouths back.

I look at the man on the sofa. His arms are folded over his body and I can see them moving up and down as he breathes. With the magazine over his face, I can't be sure if he's sleeping but it's the best shot we've got so I'm going in.

'I think so,' I whisper and, before I get too scared and change my mind, I move across the glass door and try the handle. I expect it to be locked but it isn't and the door slides across easily. It's smooth and quiet but, just as I have a big enough gap to squeeze through, a gust of wind blows across the garden and into the house. It makes a pile of papers on the floor rustle and I'm sure the professor   will   hear and take the magazine off

119

his face to see what's going on. I duck back behind the wall and wait, my heart trying hard to jump through my mouth and my neck prickly with sweat. We wait, straining our ears for a sign he's coming to find out why the patio doors have been opened. But the only thing we hear is a single bear like snore. He must be asleep.

I give the thumbs up sign to Daisy and step through the door to go inside the Belchers' living room. I can feel my hands getting clammy and my ears are drumming like they've grown their own tiny hearts.

Daisy follows me in and gently slides the door shut behind her.

So far, the plan is going well. Billy and Frankenstein are out, Barrington Belcher is fast asleep and we've managed to get over the first hurdle. We're in the house. In here, there is the same strong smell of fruit and vanilla and caramel I noticed when all the pots were bubbling last time we were here. Again, I think how strange this is. It smells just like a sweet shop. Just like Cherry McPhizz's Sweet Emporium. Suddenly all the cogs in my brain start whirring together, moving memories around and fitting them into a neat puzzle.

Sweet smells. Cherry McPhizz's huge hat and glasses. The sugar mouse. Miss Philer from the dentist. Her familiar face. Was it familiar because she looked a lot like someone else? A certain sweet shop owner perhaps?

It's such an awful thought but it fits together so perfectly that I'm sure I've just solved a huge part of the mystery. I stop dead and Daisy knocks into me.

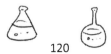

'Careful!' she hisses.

'Did Miss Philer give you a sweet when you left the dentist? You know, the day your spots appeared?' I whisper.

Daisy looks confused for a moment and then it's almost like a lightbulb has flicked on in her brain and she opens her eyes wide and nods enthusiastically.

'Sweets!' she says and I know she understands.

We creep past the sleeping professor and edge to the door. As we get there, he turns over on the sofa and the magazine falls off his face and crumples to the floor. We don't wait to see whether this has woken him up. We step out of the room and freeze on the other side, stopping to listen. The quiet snorey breathing starts up again. He's still asleep.

I point upstairs and then at myself to show Daisy that I'll look up there for Catt. Then I point to her and to the rooms downstairs.

Daisy nods and goes into the first room and I go to the stairs and begin to climb.

Chapter 22

A Dog With Two Tails

At the top, I look in the first room. It stinks of bad dog breath and cheesy socks. It must be Billy's room and it's every bit as revolting as he is. He's painted the ceiling black and all the walls are covered in tatty posters of wrestlers and computer games. His bedroom is a real mess and it's really dark but I can see Catt's not in there and I don't want to hang around so I move on.

The next room is another bedroom but there's no bed in it. Instead it's crammed with weird experiment equipment; boxes, jars and all sorts of other stuff. On a peg on the wall is the green coat Barrington Belcher wears with all the pockets. I can tell Catt isn't in here either but I can't waste an opportunity like this, so I go inside for a quick snoop around.

I open one of the boxes and inside is a clear plastic bag full of jelly snakes. The next one has giant cola bottles and the third one I look into has a nest of beautiful, bright sugar mice. *I KNEW IT!*

I carefully put two of the sugar mice in the pocket of my school cardigan. The police must be able to test these and confirm what I'm already sure of. Barrington Belcher has been working with Cherry McPhizz - and probably Miss Philer too - to poison the kids in our town with evil candy. The only thing I still don't know is *why?*

There's no more time to search this room. I need to find Catt and get out of here. I turn to leave but as I do something else catches my eye. On top of another pile of boxes is a little purple notebook. It's identical to the one I stole the other day and I scoop it up quickly and put it in my pocket with the sugar mice. Then I leave the room and move along the landing to continue my search.

The bathroom is a very normal sort of bathroom with a regular bath, basin and toilet and I'm a bit disappointed. I expected it to have things bubbling in the bath and fizzing in the toilet.

That leaves only one room left to try. The door at the very end of the landing. I guess it must be Professor Belcher's room but when I open the door, I can see it's no bedroom. Instead of a bed there are lots of little cages and hutches full of guinea-pigs and rabbits. I recognise the black and white markings of Mags curled up having a nap and I give a tiny cheer inside my head. I knew she was still alive and now this is another little mystery solved. Two bigger cages have each got two cats inside, probably the ones whose pictures are on posters stuck up

123

all over lampposts. Then there's an enormous cage at the back, taking up more than half of the floor. And inside are three dogs... fast asleep. Two of them I don't recognise but the third one I definitely do.

'Catt!' I say, so delighted to have found her that I forget to whisper.

But Catt doesn't move. I feel sick with worry and rush over to the cage. There's a bolt keeping the door shut but it isn't locked. The cage is so huge I can easily climb in and I bend down to check Catt is still alive. Her furry body is warm and I feel soggy breath coming from her stinky dog mouth. The other dogs are also breathing but I can't wake any of them up. I can see that every animal here is fast asleep but this is not the only weird thing going on in this room.

One of the other dogs in the cage has ridiculously long ears and purple fur. The other has no fur at all and his skin is covered in little green spots. I check Catt and at first it looks as though nothing has happened to her, but then I see THREE tails sticking out from her bottom. I feel my own tail droop in sadness.

'What have they done to you?' I whisper into the silky fur of her floppy ears.

'Just a little sleeping potion,' says a sinister sounding voice from behind me.

I jump and look up sharply. Professor Belcher is standing in the doorway but I don't feel scared. I should do, I know that. But I'm so furious at what he's done to Catt and the other poor animals that I can only manage

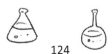

one feeling. Pure white-hot anger.

'How dare you take my dog?' I yell at him. 'What kind of person takes dogs and gives them sleeping potions for no good reason?'

'Ahh, but you're assuming I don't have a good reason,' he says with an evil smirk on his face. 'As a matter of fact, I do have a very good reason for taking your dog. It's out of the kindness of my heart.'

'Oh yeah,' I shout, still feeling completely mad. 'How do you figure that out?'

'It's quite simple really,' he says. 'I'm making new recipes for sweets every day in my laboratory and I use some ingredients that might... well, let's just say might not agree with every child who eats them. I need to test them first so I know what's going to happen.'

'But that doesn't stop you though, does it?' I say. 'When you realise your sweets are doing freaky things to kids you still give them to Cherry McPhizz to sell, don't you? And probably Miss Philer too, to give out at the dentist.'

'Of course I do,' the professor says as though I'm a total idiot. 'The Fremlin sisters pay me very good money to make sure the sweets have the effect they desire. How did they put it? Ah yes, "Maximum payment for those stinky kids."'

I have no idea what he's talking about. 'Who are the Fremlin sisters?' I ask.

'I think I've had enough of talking to you,' the professor says and he marches over and clicks a padlock

on to the cage.

'You'd better stay in there for now. Until I figure out what to do with you,' he says, backing out of the room. 'Oh, and if you're thinking of screaming or shouting then I'd think again. You see I have your dog, I have you and I have a whole house full of concoctions that could shut you both up permanently.'

The door slams behind him and all my braveness disappears. Instead of rescuing Catt, I've ended up being locked up with her. My only hope is that Daisy will get out of the house safely and fetch help before it's too late.

Chapter 23

Who Are The Fremlins?

I try to wriggle the padlock open but I don't have magic powers in my fingers so I know it's hopeless.

I lie down and curl around Catt. Even though she's still fast asleep, she's warm and familiar and this makes me feel a bit better. Something's digging into my hip and I remember the second purple notebook. This one looks older than the one I stole from the bottom of the stairs. The corners are raggy and there are little stain marks all over the cover. Three words are written on the front in tidy capital letters.

THE CANDY OPERATION

I take a look at what's written on the first page.

Clients - Miss Gertrude Fremlin and Miss Dorothy Fremlin (will   be working under the names

Miss Cherry McPhizz and Miss Felicity Philer.)

Another bit of the puzzle slots into place. The Fremlin sisters have disguised themselves as a lovely sweet shop owner and a kind dentist receptionist. And they fooled us all! I read on.

Brief - To make sweets that will taste out of this world but also make some that will have nasty effects on children

Time scale - As soon as possible

Notes - First batch discounted for local testing by the Misses Fremlin. If the project proves to be successful then will work with them to sell sweets across the country and then into Europe, America and throughout the world.

I look further into the book for more clues. There are lists of different sweets set out in columns. Information about what they taste like, which animal they've been tested on and the effects they had.

Then there are details of all those that have already been given to children. There are pages marked with details of each KAW. Juno's webbed feet, Humza's bald head, Amelie's chicken impersonation, Davey's babyish behaviour, Izzy's beard, Ryan's trombone peeing, Daisy's spots and my new tail... they're all in the book along with loads of others I don't recognise that must go to different schools.

Later in the book are lists of dates and times. Meetings with the Fremlin sisters, new batch test dates, deliveries, orders and near the back are details of new inventions. Sweets with truly awful effects, far worse than sprouting a tail or clucking like a chicken. There are horrifying details of sweets to make children shrink to the size of gerbils or turn into piglets. This all just got even more serious and I start to panic again. I wrench at the lock but the bolted door won't move at all. In a rage I kick out at it and let out an angry *grrrrrr*.

'Don't worry Catt,' I say. 'I'll get you out of here.'

I give the cage another hoof and it bends a tiny bit. I wonder what would happen if I kick it enough times... just maybe...

But, as I'm getting ready to give it another big wallop, I hear a loud shout from downstairs.

Daisy!

Chapter 24

Breaking Out

I can hear angry voices coming through the floorboards and then footsteps marching up the stairs.

The door of the room bursts open and the professor appears, shoving a scared looking Daisy in front of him.

'Look who I bumped into trying to escape through the kitchen window,' the professor says.

'Daisy!' I say.

'Sorry Mima,' she replies and she does look really sorry for herself.

'You'd better get in there with your little friend,' says Professor Belcher and he takes a key from his pocket and opens the big cage. Daisy is shoved inside and lands on top of me. Although it's a pretty big cage, there are now three dogs and two girls inside and there's not much spare space.

'What are you going to do to us?' asks Daisy.

'That depends on how well-behaved you are,' he snarls. 'I've got some new tricks up my sleeve and they're almost ready. I think I might see if I can make your eyeballs drop out or your feet grow to the size of tennis rackets. I think that's my favourite. I've been dying to try that one out for a while.'

'You'll never get away with it.' I say.

'Oh, won't I?' says Barrington Belcher but he doesn't look at all worried. 'You're not really in a position to do anything about it are you?'

I look at Daisy who's trying to be brave but I can see her hands shaking and I know she's as scared as I am.

'I think I'll keep you here for a day or two, see if I can find a use for you but then I'll be making sure you have a good strong shot of my memory wiper before I let you go.'

'What about all the animals?' I ask, stroking Catt's ears.

'I'm not a complete monster,' he says. 'I only keep them for a few days. Then, once I've finished with them, I give them a quick shot of antidote to wake them up and I let them go.'

'Does the antidote put everything back to normal?' I ask.

'Most things,' the professor says. 'There have been a few unfortunate side effects with some of the subjects. Science can be cruel.'

I think of Kirstyn's toothless rabbit, Nibbles, and

131

Frankenstein's flashing poo. Surely he wouldn't have experimented on his own son's pet?

'That's enough chat from you both. I have work to do. And remember, not a peep from either of you or...' He doesn't finish his sentence but draws his finger along the line of his neck like some terrible villain off the telly who wants to show everyone he has nothing but evil on his mind. Then he's gone.

'Daisy, we have to get out of here,' I say, which is a bit stupid because she probably isn't planning on hanging around longer than she needs. 'Things are about to get a lot worse,' I explain. 'It's all to do with sweets. The professor is making them, and Cherry McPhizz and Miss Philer are giving them to kids.'

Daisy doesn't say anything so I carry on. 'There was another notebook and it's full of new experiments. They're really horrible, Daisy, and I think they're almost ready. If we don't stop them then kids are going to be in HUGE amounts of danger.'

'Do you still have the notebook?' she asks and I pat my pocket.

'And some of the sugar mice as evidence,' I add.

'That's got to be enough for the police to believe us now,' says Daisy. She has a go at fiddling with the lock but I know she won't manage.

'We need to kick it in,' I tell her.

We both kick as hard as we can at the door. It bends a little more.

'Again,' I say.

132

'No,' Daisy puts her hand on my leg to stop me. 'Too noisy.'

She looks carefully at the door of the cage, the hinges and the lock. She's very thoughtful and her face has that clever kind of look about it.

'What are you thinking?' I ask her.

'The weakest part of the door isn't the bit that should open,' she says. 'It's the other end, where the hinges are. Look, they've already started to bend. Just a bit of careful pressure and we should be able to pop them off completely.'

She sits on the floor and puts her feet against the door.

'Sit behind me and push your back up against mine,' she says and I shuffle awkwardly around the sleeping dogs to do what I'm told. It's always the best idea when Daisy has a plan.

I push my feet against the bars and my back against Daisy. This lets her push hard against the hinges of the cage and it doesn't take long before they start to buckle. We have a break for a few minutes to get our energy back and then we push again. The hinges spring off completely and the door falls open.

'Well done, Sunny Daise!' I say.

'Come on,' she says and climbs through the opening.

'What about Catt and the other animals?' I ask. 'We can't leave them here.'

Catt has fallen asleep again and she's far too

heavy for me to carry.

'We need to find the antidote,' she says and I think I know the best place to start.

We go to the door and Daisy opens it a crack and pokes her head through.

'All clear,' she whispers and then puts her finger on her lips.

We tiptoe out of the room and along the corridor. I point to the room where I found the boxes of sweets and the notebook and we go inside. Just like his notebook, Barrington Belcher is neat and organised. The jars and bottles lined up on shelves are all neatly labelled. We look at each one but none of them are the antidote. We look through all the boxes but they're full of sweets. No antidote there either.

'He must be keeping it downstairs,' I whisper.

And if the antidote is downstairs then that's where we need to go next.

Chapter 25

The Antidote

We creep downstairs nervously. I keep expecting Billy and Frankenstein to burst in, or Professor Belcher to come out of the living room and catch us. I know he's in the living room because the radio is still on and I can hear him singing badly to some old rock song.

'Kitchen,' Daisy mouths and I follow as she tiptoes past the living room door, which is ajar.

Cupboard by cupboard we open every door silently and peer inside. They're full of the usual kitchen type stuff but there's still no sign of any antidote and we're running out of places to look. I'm about to move out of the kitchen and try the only other room we haven't checked, if you don't count the room the professor is in, when Daisy grabs my arm. She is standing by an enormous American style fridge with both doors wide open. One half has a few old bits of food and half a bottle of milk in it. And the other half is full of little boxes. Some are labelled **High-Strength Quick-Action Sleeping Potion** some are **Memory Wiper** and others are labelled **Reset Original Settings Antidote**.

I give Daisy the double thumbs up sign but I'm not ready to smile yet. We still have to get the antidote upstairs and dish it out to all the animals. Then we need to get out of the house and call the police. And all of this without getting caught by the nutty professor. Daisy takes a box of antidote and passes it to me. I open it and see a small bag of bright pink powder nestled inside.

Daisy passes me two more boxes and shoves another two into her pocket. Then she picks up another box and shows me the label. Sleeping potion.

I shrug my shoulders and knot my eyebrows to show that I don't understand.

Daisy points towards the noise of the awful singing and I realise what she is planning to do. I'm just not really sure how she's planning on doing it.

'You go and fix the animals,' she mouths. 'And I'll...'

But before she can tell me the rest of her plan, I make the biggest mistake of our mission so far. I go to put the boxes in my pocket and one falls from my grip. As I automatically reach out to grab it, I knock into the table and a glass, that was sitting right at the edge, teeters and falls to the tiled floor with a crash loud enough to wake zombies.

'You meddling little toe-rags!' bellows a voice and

Barrington Belcher comes racing through the door with a bright red face. His arms are outstretched and he's so angry it looks as though he might burst his eyeballs right out of their sockets. He roars like a furious rhino as he gallops across the kitchen floor towards us. I stare around looking for another route of escape but there isn't one.

I see Daisy open the box in her hand and I know that we will only get one shot at this. As Barrington Belcher gets to Daisy, he reaches his arms towards her and I'm sure he's going to wring her neck. But, quick as a bullet, I launch forward and practise my very best rugby tackle to send him sprawling. I squeeze his legs together and cling on with all my strength and, although he twists and wriggles, he cannot stand up.

I can feel him trying to kick out and I know I won't be able to hold him much longer but my tail wraps around his feet like a lasso and I pull tight. I'm finding out that having a tail isn't really so bad after all.

'Get off me you stupid little girl,' he shouts, trying to lever himself up onto all fours.

Daisy is ready for him and, as soon as his face looks up, she empties the powdery blue contents of the box of **High-Strength Quick-Action Sleeping Potion** all over it.

The professor coughs and splutters for a second or two, shaking his head around to try and get rid of the powder. But it must be really strong stuff because he soon stops shaking and struggling and flops down onto the kitchen floor in a heap.

'See how you like a dose of your own sleeping potion,' Daisy says to the unconscious professor.

'Sunny Daise!' I cheer. 'That was amazing!'

'I know,' Daisy says. 'But there's no time for that now. We have to get Catt and get out of here before Billy gets back from his walk.'

I look at my watch: it's quarter to eight. That means we have fifteen minutes at the most.

This time there's no need to be quiet so we pelt upstairs as quickly as we can and go straight to the cage at the back of the animal room.

'I'm sorry,' I tell the other sleeping animals. 'We'll come back for you. But we need to get help first.'

Daisy and I take a box of antidote each. I take a generous pinch of the pink powder and carefully open Catt's mouth just enough to sprinkle it inside. Daisy copies me with the purple-furred dog and then I give a dose to the bald, spotty dog. The effect is almost instant. All three open their eyes and blink them a few times before lifting their heads. Then, very groggily, they try to stand but their legs are wobbly and they can't stay on their feet for very long.

'They just need a minute,' I say but at that precise moment the front door bangs and Daisy and I stare at each other in panic.

Billy must be home!

138

Chapter 26

Getting to the Truth

We can hear someone walking through the house and then a shout. It doesn't sound at all like Billy. It sounds like a lady who knows words I'm pretty sure should never be shouted out loud. Whoever it is must have just discovered the professor in the kitchen.

'We should make a run for it,' Daisy says.

'Come on Catt,' I call and she tries again to stand up. This time she's more successful and is able to take a few wobbly steps towards me.

By the time we get to the door of the room, Catt's much steadier on her feet but it's already too late. Someone's running up the stairs and we have nowhere to go.

'YOU!' shouts Cherry McPhizz as she reaches the top of the stairs. The lovely, smiley woman with dimpled cheeks and sunshine in her eyes has gone and the lady thundering our way is the complete opposite. Her hair is still up in a bun tied with a red ribbon, but now it looks harsh and a bit like a scary witch. Her chin looks sharper and her eyes are filled with hate.

'They're up here, Dorothy,' she calls.

Miss Philer comes running up and stands next to her sister, blocking the top of the stairs. As they walk towards us, Cherry McPhizz - or Gertrude Fremlin I suppose she's really called - pulls something from her apron pocket. It looks like a super long strawberry lace. What on earth is she going to do with that?

'I seem to remember you are quite a fan of strawberry bootlaces,' she says menacingly. 'Well let's see how you like this little beauty, developed by the poor, sweet, kind-hearted professor you so cruelly knocked out in his own kitchen.'

She flicks her wrist and the strawberry lace cracks like a whip. A picture of some mountains that was hanging on the wall falls to the ground, cut clean in half. I gulp and look at Daisy. The Fremlin sisters chuckle to each other and start to walk towards us. We have no choice but to back away until we're once again in the room with all the animals.

'Now what do we do with you two little troublemakers?' Miss Philer, or rather Dorothy Fremlin, asks.

Catt can tell they're no good and she bares her teeth and begins her low warning growl. Gertrude Fremlin cracks her strawberry whip again and it whooshes

past Catt's ear. She yelps and puts her tails between her legs. I notice that at least one of the tails is definitely shrinking and I'm cheered by that. But not for long.

'My sister and I have waited a very long time for our chance to get our own back on all you nasty little children,' Gertrude says. 'And we're not going to fail when we are so close just because of two pesky toads like you.'

'Get your own back for what?' I ask, trying to get a conversation going to give Daisy some time to think up a plan for our escape. But I find that I'm actually genuinely interested in what could have made these two women so mad they want to hurt the kids of the world.

'Do you remember Fremlin Towers?' Dorothy asks and I shake my head.

'No, of course you don't. That's because it was forced to shut when you were still in your stinking nappies. The best theme park in the whole of England with the most exciting rides. The scariest ghost train, highest drop, fastest roller coaster, twistiest tracks...' Gertrude says with a strange faraway look in her eye.

'And best doughnuts,' adds Dorothy.

'So, what happened to it?' I ask.

'What happened to it?' Gertrude hisses, snapping out of her daydream. 'I'll tell you what happened to it. **You kids** happened. With your constant whinging and complaining. *I fell out of the ghost train,*' she says in what I think is meant to be an impression of a whiney child. '*I broke my leg on the bumper cars... The laser tag game*

141

chopped my ear off...'

'*I got food poisoning from the doughnuts,*' adds Dorothy.

'Children in my day knew how to enjoy a bit of danger and excitement. But these days you're all so pathetic and it was one complaint after another until they shut us down,' Gertrude spits.

'We lost everything,' Dorothy says. 'Thanks to all those horrible kids, we had no choice but to disappear for a few years. But we came back, didn't we Gertie?'

'We sure did. It took a few little bank robberies and a change of identity but we pulled ourselves out of the gutter and now we are going to wreak our revenge on all the whinging, whining children of the world.'

I look at Daisy, thinking that now would be a very good time for her to begin her brilliant get away plan. But the look on her face tells me she has no more idea of how to get out of this one than I have.

Gertrude Fremlin digs in her pocket again and pulls out another long length of strawberry lace. She throws it at Dorothy who catches it neatly.

'Tie up these annoying little girls,' she says. 'Barrington can deal with them when he wakes up. Whenever that is. It seems you gave him a very big dose of the sleeping potion. Too much for the antidote, which means he's going to have a pretty bad head ache when he does wake up.'

'I wouldn't want to be in your shoes when that happens,' says Dorothy.

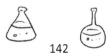

I glance at Daisy.

Dorothy pulls my hands together in front of my body and ties them tightly with the strawberry lace. Then she takes another piece and does the same with Daisy. I wriggle my hands but the lace is strong and cuts in if I move so I decide to stay still.

'The harder you struggle, the more it will hurt,' Dorothy says. 'And if you're thinking of nibbling your way through like a little mouse then be my guest. You'll find you end up with no teeth but at least you'll feel like you've tried.'

'I hope we don't have the displeasure of meeting either of you again,' Gertrude says. 'I somehow feel sure we won't!'

She cackles a truly awful laugh and Dorothy joins her. I wonder how I ever thought these women were so lovely.

Then, just when I thought things couldn't get any worse, we hear the front door open again as Billy and Frankenstein get back from their walk.

'What's going on here?' he yells from downstairs.

Chapter 27

An Unlikely Hero

I know it's only a matter of time before the crazy dog and crazier owner come up to find out what's going on. Sure enough, we hear them bound upstairs and they're soon standing in the door. Billy's face is a picture of confusion as he stares around the room.

'What's all this?' he asks.

'Ah, young Billy,' Gertrude says, putting on her fake Cherry McPhizz voice again.

'We came round to pick up some more stock for the shop and found these two intruders here.'

Billy looks at us and then at all the animals and he looks pretty surprised.

'What are these animals doing here?' he asks and now I'm the one who's surprised. How can he have been living down the corridor without knowing the room at the end was full of other people's lost pets?

'Dad told me he'd stopped all this,' he says,

pointing at the cages. 'He promised there'd be no more animals when I found him out last time.'

He turns to look at me.

'Is your dog here?' he asks.

I nod furiously.

'I asked him,' says Billy. 'I asked him outright if he'd taken her and he said no.'

'Oh dear,' says Dorothy, sticking her bottom lip out. 'Has daddy been a bad boy?'

'You really didn't know?' I ask Billy, finding it hard to believe.

'Of course not,' he says. 'You really think I'd let him do this if I knew about it?'

Daisy and I must look unsure because he snaps, 'I love animals. They're way less complicated than people. My best friend's a dog, isn't he?'

'Didn't you ever ask what he kept in this room?' Daisy asks.

'I've been walloped more than once for sticking my nose into his experiments,' Billy says. 'Soon learnt to leave well alone.'

I'm beginning to realise that Billy is not as clued up about his dad's work as we thought he was. And I suddenly get the feeling he's about to be in as much trouble as we are. I can see Gertrude coiling the strawberry whip into her hand as though she's getting ready to pounce. Her eyes narrow and she looks Billy up and down.

Just as Gertrude flicks her hand back to prepare to

strike, I yell, 'WATCH OUT!'

Billy leaps sideways out of the way at the same time as I whip my tail forward to catch the strawberry lace. I feel a searing pain tear through my tail but I can't worry about that now.

Frankenstein growls and steps towards Gertrude. She raises the whip again but she's not quick enough. Frankie springs forward and bites into her hand making her drop the lace with a yowl.

Billy grabs it and puts his hand on Frankie's collar to calm him down. I can't help being impressed.

'You need to keep that dog under control,' Gertrude screams, cradling her bleeding hand against her chest.

'Oh, I think that was very well controlled,' I say, remembering Billy's own words.

Billy looks at me and then the strangest thing of all happens. He smiles! He actually smiles. Not a nasty sneer or mean grin but a friendly, proper smile. And I smile back.

Dorothy makes a run for the door but Frankie gets there first and blocks her way, growling and showing off his sharp teeth.

'Get him out of my way,' she hisses.

'I don't think so,' Billy says. 'In fact, I think you two had better get in there where you'll be out of *our* way.'

Billy nods towards the big cage. My heart sinks for a moment but then I realise he doesn't mean us. He's talking to the Fremlin sisters.

'Of all the...' Gertrude says.

'Your father will have something to say about this,' Dorothy adds.

'I said, get in,' repeats Billy.

And, without their fearsome whip and with Frankie nudging them all the way, they have little choice but to climb into the cage, mumbling and grumbling and shoving each other as they go.

'Frankie, guard!' says Billy and the dog stands in front of the gap where the cage door would be if Daisy and I hadn't kicked it out earlier. Catt and the other two dogs, now completely awake and sensing the situation, join Frankenstein to make a wall of growling guards.

Billy comes over and undoes the knots in the laces tying our hands.

'I really didn't know about all of this,' he says. 'Honestly. I thought Dad was just making fancy sweets for them. They let me eat as many as I wanted as long as I stuck to the ones in the kitchen.'

'It's the sweets that have been making all the weird things happen to the kids,' I tell him, rubbing my wrists gratefully as soon as the laces are off. Billy looks really sorry for himself.

'What are you going to do?' he asks.

'We'll have to call the police,' I say.

'Your dad's in it pretty deep,' Daisy adds.

Billy's face crumples and he pushes his thumbs into his eyes like he's trying not to cry.

'He's not a very nice person,' he sniffs. 'Never has

147

been. He's done bad things for as long as I can remember and he's pretty nasty to me and Frankie too. But he's still my dad and I guess a bad dad is better than nothing.'

I reckon it probably isn't the right time to point out that I don't have a dad either and that I'd rather it was that way than having to live with someone like Barrington Belcher.

'I'm so sorry,' I say because I can see how painful this is for him.

'Why are you sorry?' he says looking up. 'I'm the one who's been a total idiot. I call you names, I'm always teasing you and I laugh at you when you when step in dog poo.'

'I guess that was a bit funny though,' I smile.

He smiles back.

'But I burnt your book too,' he says. 'I'm really sorry about that. I thought you were spying on me and it made me mad.'

Billy looks more sheepish than the wooliest sheep and for a moment it's difficult to link this Billy to the one who's been causing so many problems.

'Go on,' he says. 'I'll stay here with Frankie and guard these two. You go and do what you've got to do.'

And I trust him. I don't think the Fremlins were the only ones making up different identities. It feels as though this might be the first time I've seen the real Billy Belcher behind the mask of the mean bully.

I think three dogs are enough to keep the Fremlins where they are so I call Catt and we follow Daisy

148

downstairs, out of the front door and smack into Mrs Tattle who is hovering around on the front step.

Chapter 28

What About Mrs Tattle?

I scream as loudly as I can. Daisy and I have managed to escape twice already today and I'm not about to let the final member of Team Terrible capture us for a third time. If I have to, I will scream and shout until the whole of Howahorse Road comes out to see what's going on.

Daisy joins in. We both scream together and push past her out of the Belchers' garden and onto the pavement. Our screaming works and several of the neighbours come rushing out to see what all the noise is about.

'What on earth's the matter?' asks Mr Hobnob from Number 38.

'Mrs Tattle is trying to kidnap us,' I explain. 'We've only just escaped from the nutters in there.'

'We need to call the police,' Daisy says.

'I'm not trying to kidnap you,' Mrs Tattle says.

'We can't trust her,' I yell. 'She's tangled up in the whole terrible plan to cause chaos in the lives of the kids all over the world.'

'What are you on about?' says Hattie Cooper from Number 40, who has come out to see what all the yelling is about, along with several other neighbours.

'Somebody call the police,' I shout.

'But I AM the police,' says Mrs Tattle.

'Hang on,' I say. 'What?'

Mrs Tattle digs into her pocket and pulls out a walkie-talkie.

'Wow!' I say, very impressed. Daisy and I would love walkie-talkies like those.

'Back-up requested. Number 31, Howahorse Road'

She looks at us. 'Who's in there?' she asks. I'm not a hundred percent sure whether we can trust her or not but I reckon there are enough witnesses around now to back us up if needed.

'The professor,' Daisy says. 'But we gave him a sleeping potion so he's unconscious.'

Mrs Tattle raises her eyebrows at us.

'And Cherry McPhizz, and Miss Philer,' I say. 'But really they're evil masterminds called the Fremlin sisters. At the moment, they're trapped in a cage guarded by three very angry dogs.'

Mrs Tattle looks pretty impressed. 'Three adult suspects, currently detained in what appears to have been a very successful citizen's arrest.'

'Mima!' Mum says, rushing up Howahorse Road.

'Where on this earth have you been? I told you to stay close to the house and stay on our road.'

'We did,' I say truthfully.

Quite a group has assembled outside to find out what's been happening in our street. Olivia and Sid both run over to join us.

My tail is really stinging now and, when I investigate, I notice a deep gash where it caught the whip. I realise with a shock that this thing I hated so much and wanted to get rid of is now as much a part of me as my arms or legs.

'Can I borrow your scarf?' I ask Mum and she takes it off and wraps in gently around my tail.

'You poor, brave thing,' she says. 'Can you tell us what happened?'

'Yes,' Mrs Tattle says. 'I think now would be a good time for you to tell us everything you know.'

So we do. The short version for now. How we sneaked in to rescue Catt and ended up finding the notebook, the drugged animals, the boxes of sweets and all the powders we found in the fridge. I take the sugar mice from my pocket and hand them over.

'You might want to test them. I'm pretty sure you'll find they're what's been making all the strange things happen around here,' I say.

When we get to the bit about Billy and Frankenstein, Olivia and Sid look at us in amazement. For them, this is the most difficult part to believe.

'He was brilliant,' I say and Daisy agrees.

152

It's not long before three police cars screech around the corner with their blue lights flashing and their sirens wailing like really angry banshees. I always wonder why the sirens are necessary when the police pull up to the scene of the crime. Surely it's just a really great way to warn the baddies they've arrived and that they should probably clear off. The good thing about the baddies in the Belchers' house though is that, even with the loud police car warning, they won't be able to escape.

A bundle of police officers wearing protective gear jump out of the cars and rush into the open door of Billy's house.

'Ma'am,' says PC Blinkered, coming over to stand with Mrs Tattle. 'What's been going on here then?'

'These clever youngsters appear to have solved not just one mystery but two,' she says. 'They may just have got to the bottom of what has been happening to the children around here. But it seems they've also managed to track down and catch the notorious bank robbers, the Fremlin sisters.'

PC Blinkered looks at us in utter shock. 'But they're just kids,' he says. 'Are you sure?'

'Sometimes children can spot the things that are right under our noses but we fail to notice,' Mrs Tattle replies and I don't think PC Blinkered looks too happy about that.

Suddenly the buzzy chat in the street hushes as people start to come out of the house. First is Cherry McPhizz, AKA Gertrude Fremlin, held firmly on each side

by a police officer. Her bun is no longer neat but hanging off the side of her head in a messy tangle. Her mouth is drawn into a sharp straight line and her eyes are furious. She hisses at us like some sort of crazy rattlesnake and then one of the officers protects her head from the car door as the other one pushes her inside. Miss Philer, AKA Dorothy Fremlin is dragged out next and is taking a very different approach to her sister, making as much fuss and noise as she can. She keeps picking her legs up like a child so that she drops to the floor between her two captors but they don't loosen their grip and she's soon bundled into the police car next to her sister. The door is slammed on them and the car zooms away down Howahorse Road, taking them off to answer for their evil actions.

An ambulance has been called to take the, still unconscious, professor for a check up but we all know the police will be waiting by his bed when he finally wakes up.

Then Billy comes out with Frankenstein by his side. Both look lost and small and I feel really sorry for them. I wave Billy over.

'I'm really sorry,' I say and he just shrugs.

'We'll sort you out, love,' Mrs Tattle says kindly. 'You're not to worry about a thing, I will personally make sure you are very well looked after indeed. You've been a real hero today.'

We all nod in agreement and Billy smiles shyly.

'And if you think having a few friends wouldn't cramp your style too much then you can hang out with us if you like,' I say. 'You know, if you feel like it.'

Chapter 29

The Guinea Pig Village

Things get back to normal quite quickly after the professor and the Fremlin sisters are arrested. The police seize everything from the house and give out antidotes to all the KAWS. Some of them are completely back to how they were before but there are still a few shadows of the weirdness.

Humza decided to keep his bald head. He says it's much easier to be bald because he never has bad hair days anymore and his mum's happy because she doesn't have to nag him to wash it. Amelie no longer clucks like a chicken and Daisy is delighted that the green spots have disappeared. I don't tell her that sometimes, when the sun is really bright, I can still see a few marks here and there. Maybe they'll also fade in time.

Juno found she is unstoppable in swimming competitions so she decided to keep her webbed toes and Amos' teeth and tongue went back to their normal colour. Davey has stopped behaving like a baby and Izzy's beard fell out overnight. Ryan told me that the trombone noise has gone completely which he's very relieved about, but he confessed that his pee is still bright green.

And my tail? It hurt for a while but is healing nicely and I am really quite proud of it now. I don't chase it like Catt does but I do like curling it round me when I'm watching telly or going to sleep. I'll probably take the antidote at some point, but maybe not. Why get rid of something so awesome?

The animals are pretty much back to normal too. Kirstyn's rabbit, Nibbles, grew all her own teeth back which is a relief as the vet was struggling to find a set of false teeth that stayed in place.

Most of the animals are reunited with their owners, including Mags who's back at school where she belongs, although she does make a strange popping noise every now and again. For some reason the guinea pigs don't seem to have responded as well to the antidote as the other animals but nobody can figure out why. Also, a lot of them were taken from a pet shop so there's nobody to reclaim them so there are quite a few left over.

Mum says I can keep them all if I look after them. Daisy, Olivia, Siddharth and our new friend Billy are helping. Today everyone has come over to paint some of the little huts that Mum's art group made us at one of their workshops. They're all going to go in the huge, new, guinea pig village in our back garden.

The others are already busy painting when Billy arrives.

'I got you this,' he says a bit awkwardly when I open the front door. 'To say sorry for the one I burnt.'

He hands me the nicest notebook I think I've ever seen. It's really grown up with swirly patterns in green and blue all over the hard cover. It snaps shut with a magnet and it has a ribbon to mark the page.

'Wow,' I say. 'It's even got dividers to keep things organised. Thanks Billy.'

'It's not much,' he says. 'But I wanted to say sorry and... you know... thanks for being my friend.'

He shuffles from side to side looking down at the floor and his cheeks have turned the colour of strawberry juice.

'Come on,' I say, to stop his embarrassment. 'Everyone's in the garden.'

And we go out to join them.

'Pass the red,' Olivia asks. She's painting her hut to look like the post-office. Daisy's making hers into the library, Billy's painting the supermarket and I'm painting mine blue and white to look like the police station. Sid says we're all daft to be making a guinea pig village and has decided to paint his hut to look like an alien spaceship instead.

'Everyone finished with the paint?' I ask.

The guinea pig buildings and Sid's alien spaceship look brilliant. We leave them to dry in the sun and go over to play with the guinea pigs. There are eight in total

and they're all completely different. Before I had them, I thought guinea pigs didn't do much except eat grass all day long but I was wrong. Benjy, who has long blue fur, is definitely the boss. He wanders around the enclosure all day keeping an eye on what the others are up to and Sid thinks he's the best. Lily, who has four ears, is a dancer. She spins round and can even go up on her back legs. I think she's my favourite. She's so gentle and loves being stroked and cuddled. Daisy likes Bellamy best. He's only got fur on his tummy, the rest of him is smooth and bare and Daisy's Gran thinks he must be really cold so she knits him little jumpers to keep him warm. Daisy comes every day with a clean jumper for him because guinea pigs' tummies are very low down and get pretty filthy. Olivia is besotted with the tiniest of them all, a smooth-coated one the colour of milk with six legs. She calls it Marie after Marie Curie and is pretty sure she's the cleverest guinea pig in the whole village.

Billy loves them all. In fact, it turns out he wasn't kidding when he said he was a real animal lover. He's so gentle with them and they always click and chirrup when they see him. Since he was fostered by Mrs Tattle, he's become so much nicer. It's been almost two months since his dad was taken off by the police and he's spent most of that time living across the road with our nosy neighbour.

'Who wants a sandwich?' Mum asks, coming out with a big plateful and some carrots and broccoli for the guinea pigs.

158

'No thanks,' say Olivia, Daisy and Sid because they have learnt not to trust any food Mum dishes up.

'I'd love one please Mrs Malone,' says Billy, who strangely doesn't seem to mind the weird concoctions.

'Now then, Billy love, I've told you a million times you must call me Bow,' Mum says, handing the plate over.

'Mmmm,' Billy says, through a mouthful of bread. 'What's in them today?'

'Chocolate spread,' Mum says and I see Olivia lean closer as though she might change her mind.

'With tinned salmon,' Mum finishes and I laugh as Olivia snaps her hand back.

'I think I'll just stick to the lemonade thanks,' she says.

Once the sandwiches and drinks are finished, I stand up to take the plate and empty mugs back into the kitchen. Billy gets up too.

'Let me help you,' he says and I smile. I'm still getting used to this new improved version of Billy Belcher.

On the way to the kitchen he says, 'Mima, what did you do with my notebook?'

'Your notebook?' I ask, trying to work out what he's talking about.

'I know you took it. I mean it was on the stairs in my house when you came round that time to fetch your mirror thing and then, when I came back from catching Frankie, it'd gone.'

'That was yours?' I ask in surprise.

'Yeah, I thought you knew.'

'No!' I reply. 'We thought it was your dad's. All the codes in it, they were our initials.'

'You figured it out then,' Billy says, blushing.

'Well no, not really,' I confess. 'That was as far as we got. What were all the numbers and tallies and weird words about? We thought they must have been a code your dad had to show what he wanted to do to each of us.'

'No,' says Billy quietly. 'My book and my codes.'

'What did it all mean?'

'It's daft really,' he says, looking in every direction except for straight at me.

'Try me,' I say.

'I wanted friends but I found it much easier to be nasty to people.'

'But why?' I ask. 'If you'd been kinder, we'd all have been friends with you I'm sure.'

'Dad reckoned I wasn't the right sort of person to have friends,' Billy says with a shrug. 'I guess if I didn't try then nobody could prove him right.'

'Oh Billy!' I say, suddenly understanding a bit more.

'Also, I could never have had proper friends anyway in case they wanted to come round. Which could never have happened because of all the weird stuff dad had going on in the house.'

'What does all this have to do with your

notebook?' I prompt.

'The book was a list of all the people in the class that I liked and what would be nice things to do if we were friends.'

I picture Billy sitting in that horrible room, writing in his book on his own every night whilst his dad was busy making evil sweets and I feel so sad for him.

'You wrote *dogs* by my name,' I say.

'Yeah, I knew you had a dog and I thought it might be fun to have someone to take Frankie out with.'

'It had nothing to do with my tail?'

'No. Just dog walking.'

'We could do that this afternoon,' I say. 'All of us.'

'Really?' Billy says.

'Sure! We all love Frankie, now he's stopped trying to eat us,' I say. 'Besides there's only one more week of the summer holidays left so we should really make the most of it. Let's bring some snacks and a blanket and we can have a mini picnic.'

The others love the idea and we spend a happy couple of hours on the common, throwing balls for Catt and Frankie, and chatting in the sun.

***

When we get home there's a huge lorry outside Billy's old house. All the potions and science stuff went ages ago but now the furniture is being loaded up. We watch two men carry the huge dog cage out of the house and I

feel Billy shiver.

'Did you get all your stuff out of there?' I ask.

'Not much worth keeping really,' says Billy.

'Are you okay?' Sid asks.

Billy shrugs. 'It's not like I have much choice,' he says.

'I guess not,' says Daisy.

'It never felt like home anyway,' Billy adds sadly and we all pile in for a group hug.

Billy's one of us now. After all, he helped us escape one mad bad inventor and two evil sisters, and he helped rescue Catt and all the other animals. He's also pretty good with a paintbrush!

I have no idea who will be moving in next door when the house is sold, but I do know that I am ready for anyone because I have the best friends ever and together, we can take on anything.

163

ACKNOWLEDGEMENTS

I'm very lucky to be surrounded by a lot of amazingly wonderful and supportive folk, and it's them who have made this happen.

An enormous thank you - bigger than that - THANK YOU is owed to my tremendous writing friends.

Fiona, Meredith, Donna, Clare, Carry and Karla – my posse of wonder who have done so much more than critique. You hold me up on this crazy journey and you catch me every time I fall. I couldn't be without you.
Andy and Vashti, I am in awe of all you have achieved and I am beyond grateful that you have given me your time and support (not to mention your fab cover quotes!)

To my extended family of kid lit folk. Thank you for the parties, the launches, the ear bending, the support and, most of all, the friendships. Especially to Jo Clarke, Tizzy Frankish and Jules Bryant. Watch out for these beauties, they are the award winners of the future.
Thank you to the brilliant Aimee Hayes who took the time to edit and polish Mima's story. And to the very clever Jag Lall for the awesome cover.

To the wonderful forces that are SCBWI and FCBG. Both organisations have led to some great friendships as well as the opportunity to swaddle myself in children's books.

164

And finally, my family. Will, you give me the tools I need to write. Mum and Dad, you give me the encouragement I need to carry on. And my not so little babies, Lily and Jemima, you give me a constant supply of inspiration and quirky, funny story starters. I love you all.

A gentle furry nudge at my foot has reminded me to add my thanks to Pippi dog. After all, no story can be written with cold feet and Pip makes sure mine are always toastie.

Printed in Great Britain
by Amazon